The RANGER of the

SUSQUEHANNOCK.

We Came to Chasms That We Vaulted and Pools That We Circled

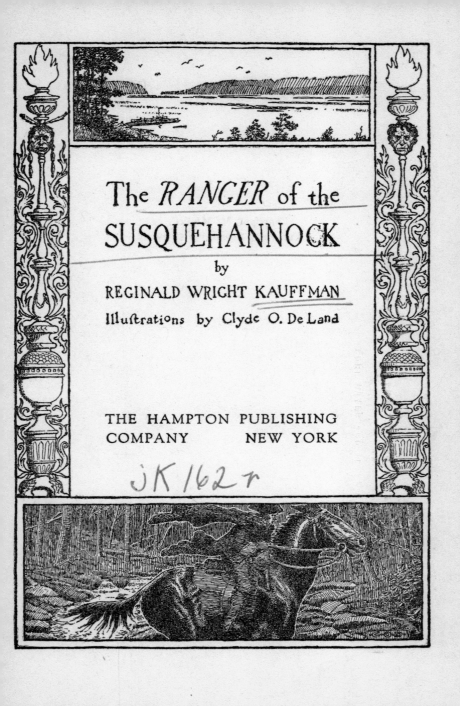

The *RANGER* of the SUSQUEHANNOCK

by

REGINALD WRIGHT KAUFFMAN

Illustrations by Clyde O. De Land

THE HAMPTON PUBLISHING
COMPANY   NEW YORK

The Camp of the Marylanders.

Table of CONTENTS

CONTENTS

The *RANGER* of the SUSQUEHANNOCK

CHAPTER I

THE BLACK CLOAK

HIS day is the 25th of October, 1781. Five years ago, my elder son, Geoffrey, was killed at my side when, under General Mifflin, we fought Rall's Hessians in the Battle of Trenton; but he left behind him as fine a boy as this new country of ours can boast. Frank, my second son, survives, and has two lads and a girl waiting his return from the wars, in the new house at Hempfield, on the Susquehanna. There Mad Anthony Wayne has sent me, because, if you please, I am sixty-odd and got a scratch in his service! And there, having just received news that Lord Cornwallis surrendered on the 19th inst., I propose to write down for my grandchildren how it came about that I, their fathers' father, born in England under the Hanoverian king, George I, came to be a loyal citizen of these American Colonies which, by God's grace, will henceforth owe allegiance to no foreign power and will acknowledge no government save such as they themselves elect.

To do this, I must tell a stormy story with more bloodshed in it than I hope my grandchildren will ever see through their own eyes. I must tell of the Pimpled Man and the slavers, of the highwayman on the Wilderness Road, and of how I was sold for the sum of £2, sterling. There is the contents of my Uncle Simon's strong-box to be revealed, as I spied it by the light of a flickering candle in the shadowy attic. There is the hammering on the door in the dead of that wild night when I began my adventures with an outlaw; the race in the darkness from Lancaster, the pistol-play at the river, the mystery of Cresap, and the murder of Knowles Daunt.

Fight follows fight, and pursuit is always close to capture. The Border-War, my imprisonment at the hands of our enemies, and peril by flood and fire all have their place in this history. I am gray-haired now, but when I tell you of them I become again the boy that I was when they happened: the boy whose first knowledge of America began on that leaden morning in the Seventeen-thirties when the full-rigged immigrant-ship *John and Anne* (Rotterdam to Philadel phia; Thos. Warcut, Master) was creeping through an oily sea just out of sight of Cape Henlopen.

In the Low Countries, the *John and Anne* had shipped 350 settlers for William Penn's Colony; at Plymouth, she picked up a score more, of whom I, travelling by myself, the only lad aboard, was one. To-day—after a three months' voyage—scarce sixty of all those passengers remained alive.

I never knew a more grievous journey—no, nor a more grievous time, not even that winter, years later, at Valley Forge. The plague swept the ship, the food was famine-rations, and wormy, too. The immigrants who had set sail as freemen were treated little better than slaves. Their belongings had been left lying on the Rotterdam docks, to make room for freight that paid Master Warcut a higher figure, and this bully of a captain, ever supported by his wolfish first-mate Grimshaw, charged us all so dearly for the bare necessities of life that most of us were hopelessly in debt to him.

I looked about me, on this morning, and saw only a scene of desolation and despair. Most of the travellers were too ill or starved to come on deck, but here and there a few crouched against the rail, while others, having staggered out of the dark quarters below and fallen from sheer weakness, lay quiet or moaning in the path of sailors, who kicked them aside. At my right, in the prow, stood a tall figure wrapped in a vast black cloak

which the wind beat with loud drummings behind him
—the only passenger that showed no ill effects from our
voyage. At my left, there rose now, above a hatch-
way, the pale face and staring eyes of Hagenbach, a
kindly Swiss immigrant, to whom I had, on embarking,
entrusted for safe-keeping the £10 passage-money
which, like the rest of us, I should have to pay so soon
as we reached Philadelphia.

Hagenbach tottered toward me and clutched one of
my arms with his skinny fingers. He had attended the
University of Basel and commonly spoke English with
me; but now he was both so enfeebled and so enraged
that I could not at once understand the sounds he made.

"Have you—have you heard?" he began and then
lapsed into mere mouthings.

As gently as I could, I tried to quiet him.

"Have I heard what?" I at last inquired.

He leaned against me, panting heavily.

"This latest cruelty of that beast?—It may well be
the last, for it will kill the most of us!"

There was no need to ask whom he meant: on the
terrible *John and Anne,* when man or woman spoke of
a wild beast they referred to no one except the ship's
captain. So:

"What has Master Warcut done now?" I asked.

And the sick Swiss told me:

"He has raised the price of bread to a shilling a loaf."

Boy though I was, I understood the result of that:

10

the already half-starved immigrants must surrender most of their remaining coppers or starve entirely.

" Are you certain? " I demanded.

" With my own ears," said Hagenbach, " I heard the mate Grimshaw give it as Warcut's order."

The eyes of my poor friend followed mine to the deck-house close beside the mainmast amidships, where, when he had worked one deviltry, Captain Warcut—sometimes with his fellow-demon Grimshaw, but more often alone—would shut himself to drink strong waters and meditate new outrages.

" We dare not petition him," gasped the Swiss.

For my part, I thought that we must, and said so. The man should have some spark of justice remaining in him.

" Let us," pleaded Hagenbach, " first appeal to the Stranger."

That was the name by which we all knew the mysterious tall man of the black cloak at present standing in the prow. His real title or purpose nobody on that accursed ship was aware of.

Wrapped to the chin, and with his dark plumed hat drawn low over his face, he had come aboard from a little skiff in Plymouth harbor, during the twilight of early dawn, just after our sails were set. Throughout the horrors of the voyage, he kept himself apart, scornful of us all: of miserable immigrants, cursing sailors and bullying commander, of plague and famine—aye, and of death. He slept on deck, swathed ever in his great cape. The winds might blow it free of his legs, but it was always tight above his chin, and no breeze raised the shadow of his hat: none of us had yet fully seen his face. In his neighborhood, the passengers felt themselves close to a person of some superior position; the crew regarded him with superstition, and Captain Warcut himself, who had never a word with him, must have been impressed by his bearing, for he avoided the Stranger as if afraid this traveller could lower him in the eyes of his subordinates.

I shared in some degree the common awe, but here was no time to indulge it. Drawing Hagenbach by the sleeve, I advanced and, raising my cap, accosted the cloaked figure.

" Sir," said I, " we are in trouble."

The Stranger did not turn. He spoke with his gaze still on the waters through which the ship was ploughing.

" Trouble," he said, " is nothing new to any man aboard this scurvy vessel."

Under his cloak his shoulders shrugged, after the French fashion, and I felt Hagenbach sigh in despair. Nevertheless, I spoke straight at the Stranger's back, keeping my voice as firm as possible, and told him what had happened.

When I had ended, there was a moment's silence. I thought that the gentleman disdained further speech with us, but presently, though still without turning, he inquired:

" Was the price of bread mentioned in your contract before sailing? "

I looked at Hagenbach, who shook his weary head.

" No, sir," said I.

" Why, then," came the Stranger's voice, as if from the folds of his cape, " where lies your complaint? I can help not at all, my lad, unless this dog breaks a contract or violates a law."

His tone was cold, and there was that in it which forbade discussion. I flushed at the rebuff, but could only lead Hagenbach away.

" You see," I said, " we must lodge our protest with the captain."

My friend held aloof, but I at last persuaded him. I, too, was timid, yet hid my timidity, for I knew that right was upon our side and that, moreover, to show weakness to Hagenbach would be to increase his own terrors.

We walked to the deckhouse, and there I knocked boldly on the door.

CHAPTER II

MUTINY ON THE HIGH SEAS

THE deckhouse door was flung open with startling suddenness. At his back a table with a bottle and a glass on it, Master Warcut stood there, the doorknob in one burly hand, glowering in our direction out of bloodshot eyes.

I stepped within, Hagenbach shambling after me. Saying never a word, the captain slammed the door and knitted his heavy brows at us.

Thomas Warcut has gone to his grave these many years ago, and I pray God's mercy on his soul; but he was a hard and greedy man, unscrupulous and savage, nor to this day can I remember him without anger. He had a leering, storm-bitten face, with a long, ragged scar running down one cheek, the left, I think, and fierce red moustaches. In all weathers he wore sea-boots, into which his trousers were stuffed carelessly. He was short, but very broad of shoulder, and, as we now saw him, his hairy chest covered only by a sleeveless and unbuttoned undershirt, his arms hung menacingly—the heavy-muscled, corded arms of a blackamoor, ending in fists that were twin sledge-hammers.

Perhaps he thought to terrorize us by his silence.

14

Me he did scare; but, queerly enough, the sickly Hagenbach found bravery now that there was no retreating.

"Master Warcut," says he, "we have come to protest against the rise in the price of bread."

The captain's face went purple.

"What business is that of yours?" he demanded, and he looked at his pistols, on a near-by shelf.

Our danger was evident, but I swelled with pride at the manner in which my friend met it. Enfeebled as he was, he yet gave the fellow eye for eye.

"Business?" said he. "It is a life-or-death business."

They were the last words he ever did say.

"Then let it be death!" bellowed Master Warcut.

Like a bolt of lightning, his mighty right arm shot out from its shoulder. The sledge-hammer fist smashed full between poor Hagenbach's eyes.

The sick man fell. He did not first totter; he did not crumple: he fell his length with a crash, his head striking the table-edge—and there lay on the deckhouse floor, bloody, motionless.

It required no experience to tell me what had come to Hagenbach.

"You've killed him!" I cried.

For answer, Warcut grasped me by the collar of my jacket and threw me bodily some several feet across the cabin. I hit the wall and collapsed into momentary unconsciousness.

When I raised my lids, the captain was taking something from the dead man's clothes. It was the passage-money that I had given Hagenbach for safe-keeping.

"That's mine!" I said, struggling to my feet. My voice was a whisper, but I was no longer afraid.

Warcut stowed the money into a trouser-pocket.

"Anything found on the body of an immigrant dying at sea belongs," said he, "to the ship's master." He smiled: with murder at his feet and that stolen money in his pocket, he leered at me.

I was only a defenseless lad: what did I matter? I knew it ran in his mind that I was not worth a blow, which knowledge, and the realization of the foul deed done to Hagenbach, still further roused me. I was resolved that, when we reached port, the captain should swing for this day's work, but I was resolved to get my £10, too. I staggered to the table and leaned on it.

"The money is mine," I repeated. "He"—I nodded to the still form on the floor—"was keeping it safe for me."

Warcut poured himself a dram. He drank slowly, eyeing me over the glass.

"Safe!" he mocked, between swallows. "You will have to prove property, and who are you to do that against a man of my standing?"

There he brought me up short. Who was I, indeed? A motherless boy, whose father was a life-prisoner in the Tower of London!

I could have told him this and, when the brute laughed at it, could have told him of the helpful influence that, I was sure, awaited my arrival in Philadelphia. But, though young, I was no fool. Once Thomas Warcut learned of my uncle's position in Pennsylvania, he would know himself to be in my power, and that my evidence would send him to the gallows for Hagenbach's murder. If he continued to believe me friendless, he might spare me, report the Swiss dead of the plague and either mock my accusations or endeavor to buy my silence—whereafter I, safe ashore, could denounce him to the law. But should I reveal my connections, why then I should never leave this deckhouse alive: I should die here of the same sudden malady that had stricken my companion.

I hung my head, really to hide my anger, but, as he supposed, to cover my defeat.

The captain held the door partly open. It was enough for my exit, but not enough to reveal Hagenbach's body to anyone that might be passing along the deck.

" Get you gone! " he snarled. " And if ever you say a word of what has happened here, it will be over the ship's side with you! "

He drew a little away from me, and I started to go; but just as I dodged by him, my eye caught the gleam of a piece of money on the floor. I guessed it to be a portion of my ten pounds, which had slipped through his thick fingers and fallen, unheeded by us both, in the shock of my discovery of his theft. The sight of some of my own property at that rogue's feet was too much for my discretion. I stooped, seized the coin and only then darted outside.

I was quick; but I had not gone six paces before he had me. I heard his boots slam twice; immediately one of his hairy hands re-collared me, and his face, purple again with rage, bent over mine so close that the breath of his drunken fury grilled my cheeks.

"Now, you young thief," he shouted, "*you will pay!*"

I wriggled; I cried out. But my captor held me in his grip as securely as the jaws of a terrier hold a captured mouse.

I cast one frenzied look about me. The deck was all but deserted. A couple of immigrants lay or sat where I had last seen them; but they looked at us without motion, too weak or too frightened to interfere. The Stranger had left the prow; he was beside the rail, not far distant and fronting us; yet (though his face was hidden as always) his folded arms and uninterested attitude indicated as much disdain for my plight as he had felt for all the other tragedies of our voyage.

"Help! Help!" I cried.

Warcut swore and shook me until my teeth rattled. I could not mistake his intention. My seizure of that piece of money had shown him that he had not conquered me, and so he was resolved to send me after Hagenbach.

" Murder! " I shrieked.

Then my wind was stopped, for the captain's free palm closed over my opened mouth. He started to drag me into the deckhouse. A roll of the ship set the door wide, and within one could see the sliding corpse of the Swiss. I gave myself up for lost.

Yet that widening of the door was the best plea for me. The Stranger must have observed what had befallen Hagenbach and have drawn a right conclusion of what it was intended should occur to me. His left hand went to his hat, pulling it still farther over his brows; his right, as he leaped forward, fell on the captain's broad shoulders and fell, I am sure, not lightly.

" What is this? " he asked.

Warcut could only snarl.

I twisted until my mouth was uncovered.

" He has killed my friend," I gasped, " and taken my money! "

" The Dutchman fought me," swore Warcut with an ugly oath, " and this boy's a thief! "

But my courage had returned again.

" Hold him! " I screamed.

The Stranger pinioned Warcut's arms. In an instant, I had recovered all of my ten pounds. Then my defender pushed me behind him and pushed the captain so hard before that he was saved a fall only by tumbling against the deckhouse wall.

I know not why Warcut had stood so long in awe of this one of the passengers, unless it was the instinctive respect of a bully for a gentleman; but now his rage overcame any other emotion. The captain's face went from purple to a more terrifying white. He had come without his pistol, but he jumped for the mainmast and seized a belaying-pin.

"*Mutiny!*"

He bawled it at the top of his lungs.

There was an answering pound of feet on the deck. Spying from behind my protector, I could see the crew gathering from their duties. Most of them were running forward out of the forecastle, and at their head was wolfish Grimshaw, the mate.

"*Mutiny!*" bawled Warcut a second time and raised the belaying-pin high.

Being still behind the Stranger, I could not see all that he did; but he acted unhesitatingly. His cloak was tossed backward on either side. As he drew his sword, I caught the flash of the blade, and immediately I knew that its point was against Warcut's hairy chest.

"Stand away, my lads!" called my protector to the onrushing crew, and I could have wagered that there was a sort of joy in his ringing voice. "Stand away, unless you prefer a dead captain to a live one!"

20

They obeyed him, for all too clearly he meant what he threatened.

" And now," quoth he to the captain, " remember that when you deal with me, Master Warcut, you are dealing with no foreign peasant, nor yet with a weak lad: you are dealing with an English gentleman.—Come on, you dog, if you dare!"

CHAPTER III

THE PIMPLED MAN

HERE it is high time that I answer for you the question that I durst not answer Butcher Warcut. I must tell you who I was and how I was ever unlucky enough to come aboard the *John and Anne:* I was Nicholas Rowntree, only child of Francis James Rowntree, that Lord Ravenscar whose estate of Whitby Wyke lay along the German Ocean's cliffs in the North Riding of Yorkshire, England, during those days when the last reigning member of the House of Stuart sate upon the British throne.

Lord Ravenscar's story made talk and to spare in his time, but now it is largely forgotten. My father, like all our family before him, remained true to the Stuart cause. The Whig Party, who supported the usurper, hated us and, on the discovery of one of the many plots to bring back the true king (whom they called the Chevalier de St. George) they forced Ravenscar to flee to Italy, where his royal master was then living in Rome.

I was a mere baby, my father having married late in life, and of these events I know only what I have been told; but certain it is that my father's title was declared forfeit and that, in some manner, his lands—and the old

22

Wyke Castle among them—passed into the possession
of his stepbrother, my Uncle Simon Scull, who had
prudently taken no part in the politics of that day.
My mother and I, unable to escape with my father, remained as Uncle Simon's guests.

Of that uncle, as he was during my father's first
absence, and indeed for all the period that I dwelt in
Wyke Castle, I retain almost no memory, and I am
grieved to add—so soon do little folk forget those whom
they were happier to remember—not much of my gentle
mother. I keep, nevertheless, in my mind the picture
of sweet gray eyes beneath level brows and a pair of
lips at once the saddest and the bravest that ever I knew,
and I have still at my old ears the echo of her low voice.
Many's the night when, none else being nigh, I was sung
to sleep, not by the peaceful ballads familiar to most
nurseries, but with the marching-songs of the Cavaliers
and the crude, heart-stricken ballads of defeated Jacobites, one in particular of which—called, I think, " The
Lass O' Morven "—runs in my head to this distant land
and time:

> " ' Far away is he I love,
>   And who shall watch above him?
> Here are only those who hate—
>   And who is there to love him?
> Yet I wadna ' (vows the Lass)
> ' Hae him aught but frae me,
> While the land that bore my love
>   Bears no love for Jamie! ' "

And then quickly shifting from sorrow to a high defiance, this refrain:

> " Over the water to Jamie—over the water to Jamie!
> Stand, and we'll sing:
> ' Here's to the King—
> The King that is over the water!' "

However, we lived, you are to suppose, much as hundreds in our position were then living, and so matters stood until my eighth birthday.

That night, my father reappeared. I recall how I was brought down from my bed to be kissed by the big, laughing man whose strong embraces frightened me so that I all but cried; how my uncle left the Castle, saying he must seem to have no knowledge of Lord Ravenscar's presence in it; and how, a few hours later, I was awakened by the loud entrance of the Hanoverian soldiers. Somebody had betrayed my father to them, and they came to take him away.

I had tiptoed down in my nightshift and bare feet. None saw me as I stood trembling on the stairs, to the foot of which my parents had withdrawn for a farewell word together. The candles were lighted in the great hall, and it was filled with armed men.

I heard my father whisper to my mother:

" Tell Simon where I have hidden them and bid him keep them safe for our King."

I would have asked of what he spoke, but at this

24

moment the leader of the soldiers bade the speaker accompany him.

Of the parting that followed I have no heart, even now, to tell. My father was carried away, and soon I learned that he had been arrested not only for his past Stuart plots, but on the charge of having returned to England to secure for his exiled monarch something which, appertaining to the royal family, had been concealed in the flight of the Stuarts, years before, and never discovered by the Hanoverian usurpers.

The rest, so far as I then knew it, is soon told. Lord Ravenscar was thrown into the Tower of London. He escaped execution, largely, I think, because so long as he lived, they hoped to get from him certain Stuart secrets, but he was kept in close confinement: we could not communicate with him. Very shortly and speedily, Uncle Simon sold the estates and went to Mr. William Penn's Colony in Pennsylvania, where we heard that he rose to a place of some influence. My mother (pining for my father so sorely that she could not speak freely to me of these matters) died of a broken heart, and I was taken care of, for five years, by a neighboring widower, Squire Wedgewood, of Ayton. He, too, was now dead. His nephew, who inherited his lands, had no acquaintance with me and no reason to burden himself with my care. By one ship, he sent a letter to my Uncle Simon, whose very features I had forgotten, saying that I was coming out to America by the vessel following; then, giving me only the £10 passage-money, and enough besides to provide for my bare subsistence on the voyage, he put me aboard that next ship —and it was the *John and Anne*.

So here I stood behind the Stranger, and there stood the Stranger with his blade at Master Warcut's breast, and what Master Warcut's face then looked like I should have been glad to see.

For a moment he said nothing. Then, in a surly voice, he cursed his men.

" Get you back to your quarters! " cried he.

The crew, still headed by Grimshaw, slowly retired.

" Well, dog? " asked the Stranger, never lowering his sword.

" Will you cry quits? " countered Warcut. " Will you pass your word to say naught of all this? "

The Stranger laughed openly. " It is for the victor to offer terms," he said, " and I offer nothing."

The captain was a thorough blackguard, but some pluck he had, and now he showed it.

" You have the upper hand to-day," he growled, " but I warn you: so soon as we reach land, I shall give you over to the law on a charge of mutiny."

He turned his back to the sword and passed into the deckhouse. The Stranger sheathed his blade and, wrapping his cloak about him, walked straight to the boat's prow, whither he beckoned me.

Nothing loath, I followed.

THE PIMPLED MAN

" We must camp here," he said, " and, turn by turn, keep an eye on these rogues."

That we did throughout the brief remainder of the voyage. I watched while he slept, which was little, and he while I slept, which was much.

But nothing happened. In the first night, Warcut and Grimshaw weighted poor Hagenbach's body and threw it overboard to the accompaniment of no prayers save such as were muttered by my protector and me. Next day, we bribed an immigrant, a Lancashire trades-man, to bring us food. The crew left us alone; the mate only scowled; the captain would not look at us, and, all this while, despite our common danger and our close companionship, the Stranger's face was never wholly shown me. I realized only that he was dark, with brilliant eyes and the nose of an aristocrat: he did his best to hide his countenance both when awake and napping, and his meals he took with his head averted. So the *John and Anne* made speed, under fair winds, along the remainder of the coast and up the Delaware, and so, also, as the sun was setting one evening, she came in sight of the town of Philadelphia and finally anchored off what I learned later was Anthony Milkin-son's Wharf.

A boat put out from shore and came toward us. My boyish curiosity, as well as my concern for the Stranger, impelled me to lean over the rail far forward, where we still held our ground, and to watch this craft's advance.

In answer to hails from the ship, the boat made for our starboard side and, as to do so she must cross our bows, I got a good view of those she carried.

They seemed all, save one, men either of arms or of some civil dignity. That one sat clutching the side, as if fearful of a capsizing, and him I somehow viewed with repulsion.

He was a lean person who, I guessed, would be stoop-shouldered even in his most erect position, and he was clad in a suit the color of iron-rust. He raised his face as the boat passed beneath me: it was a clean-shaven, pale face, as white as parchment where it was not crowded with pimples, and yet therewith so very crowded that I wondered how the razor could find a bloodless way among them. Our eyes met, and his, I saw, were red and bleared.

There were callings to and fro, shouted inquiries from the boat as to our voyage, and especially from the *John and Anne's* officers as to the news of some band, as it appeared of Pennsylvania outlaws, whom they called " Cresap's Men," and of whom I was to learn enough later. Hastily, I drew my gaze away from him of the pimples and considered his companions. I made no doubt that these were the port-authorities.

" What," I inquired of the Stranger, " will you do now, sir? "

He had seemed to be giving the boat no attention. He slipped one of his smooth hands under his cloak.

" For me there is no hurry," said he, " but what of you? "

That he might well ask, for no sooner had the boat got alongside and her half-dozen men swarmed aboard of us than a murmur of dismay ran through the group of emaciated immigrants, who promptly huddled up to the port-officers on the side of the crowd opposite to that on which stood Captain Warcut. The passenger that had been bringing us food ran to the Stranger and me.

" The beast demands £12 for his passage-money! " cried this fellow. " Twelve—and he bargained for but ten when we embarked! "

The Stranger shrugged.

" How may even Warcut do that? " I asked.

Our messenger shook his head. " He says it is because the voyage was longer than he had computed— and Heaven knows it has been overlong! He says that whoso lacks the odd two pounds may land only if he bind himself as a servant to one of the planters from the interior—they have journeyed to Philadelphia to secure just such slaves. I have enough money left, but these other poor men—I believe it was all secretly agreed on before ever we set sail for this accursed country! "

He ran back to hear more of it, and the Stranger turned to me.

" I will lend you the additional money," said he.

But I thanked him and told him there was no need. I had, I said, an uncle that was to meet me, a man of substance, well able to defray every charge and rescue me under the nose of the captain's possible accusations.

"You must think of yourself, sir," said I. "Watch Warcut! What will *you* do?"

I had scarce put the question before there was a movement among the officers, and heads were directed toward the pair of us.

"Perhaps my uncle ——" I began.

"What is your uncle's name?" asked the Stranger.

But he received no answer, for at that instant, Captain Warcut ended something that he had been saying, and pointed us out, shouting:

"And there stands the mutineer!"

What followed happened in a trice. I saw the immigrants and the Pimpled Man draw back out of harm's way. I saw the port-officers rush toward us, Grimshaw putting himself at the head of them, and Warcut outdistancing even Grimshaw, the leer of triumph on his face, a cocked pistol in his hand. Then the Stranger shoved me aside, whipped off his cloak, bound it deftly about his middle and leapt at the lot of them.

The attackers were attacked. The captain was now well ahead: before he could fire, the Stranger had thrust a dagger between the ribs of that murderous hound and tossed his body over the side as he himself, with Grimshaw's help, had flung Hagenbach's. Then, with amaz-

ing agility, the avenger vaulted to the rail, turned about
on it and stood poised there.

He swept his hat to the stupefied crowd. I had my
glimpse of his full face now—swarthy, handsome, an
exulting demigod.

"Gentlemen," he cried in the very eyes of those
dumbfounded officers, " I thank you for my welcome to
your City of Brotherly-Love! "

CHAPTER IV

UNCLE SIMON

THE thing, I have said, was effected in a trice, and to be sure only so could it have been accomplished. Speed did it. One instant the Stranger was disposing of Warcut, the next he was balanced on the ship's rail, and the third he had plunged head-foremost overboard and was hidden by the evening cloud-shadows in the bosom of the Delaware.

Freed of his presence, port-officers and crew recovered their courage. While he faced them, they were figures of stone; no sooner was his back turned than they imitated his promptitude. With the wolfish mate for leader, they flocked to the side; they discharged their pistols into the twilight—but into nothing else. You would have said then that there never were braver fellows, but their daring was too tardy: the body of the captain was, as I heard, recovered on the morrow; his slayer seemed not to have been hit in the water, nor was he later heard of in the town.

For my part, I of course rejoiced in his escape, but he was scarce gone before I had cause to understand that his safety became my danger. The avengers soon gave up the comedy of firing at nothingness, and Grimshaw, balked of his death-feud, turned from the rail and

came toward me, where I stood far forward still trans-
fixed like a boy on his first visit to the theatre or a
man that has seen a miracle.

The fellow's head hung low; his mouth opened in a
nasty fashion, and, from under his matted hair, his eyes
shone cold and covetous. I realized then that I was
now alone and friendless aboard the *John and Anne*:
that the mate must have learned from Warcut my possession of the £10, that he meant to have the money
out of me, and that to get it he would denounce me, as
his master had done, for a thief. Though I looked at
him unable to tear my gaze from his, what I saw there
was not only this malevolent ruffian: I saw myself in
a loathsome prison-cell—I saw even the scaffold, and
the gallows on it.

" Come here," Grimshaw ordered, and he beckoned
with a crooked forefinger.

I had a mind to follow my protector and fling myself
upon the mercy of the river, but he read my purpose
and laid his icy grip about my wrist. I faced him with
(I trust) enough show of courage, but with a very
certain terror in my breast.

" Let me go! " I cried. And then I added: " You
coward! "

" Coward? " says he. " There's never a soul has
called me that and long survived! "

He gave my wrist a bitter wrench. My heels dug
into the deck. In vain: without another word to me,

he dragged me amidships toward the port-officers, now each excusing his own conduct and blaming his comrades', and toward the Pimpled Man in rusty clothes, who, though he had taken no part in the armed hostilities, was reappeared among the crowd and assumed, it would seem, some degree of authority.

" The lion has shown us his heels, but," says Grimshaw, with an oath that made me start, " here's his cub! "

Immediately their angered faces encircled me: that group of sturdy men, and I a lonely, lanky lad, sallow by nature, emaciated from privation and I fear confessing at last, in my brown eyes, the dread in which I stood of them.

" This whelp," pursued the mate, " was that pirate's go-between with the immigrants: he and a Swiss that we had to kill were the agents that fomented the mutiny."

I could see how it would be with me: thwarted in their major hatred, the officers were quick to feel and eager to satisfy a minor enmity. They had lost the chief criminal, and that exposed them to the censure of their superiors ashore; but they could lessen the blame if they arrested his lieutenant. I was their partial justification, and so they were ready to believe anything against me. I looked wildly from one to another: only the stooping Pimpled Man kept his head, and yet his unbelieving smile appeared nearer to contempt than indifference.

"Why," says he, peering at me with a quick, sharp look, "it's a mere boy!"

This was no great encouragement, but it was something, and I resolved to make the most of it. I dragged at Grimshaw's arm that held me. Could I have freed myself there is no telling what I would have done.

"Sir," I gasped, "if you will let me speak one word ——" U. S. 653172

Then my protest was suspended as if a hand had been clapped upon my mouth: the Pimpled Man (he had the nose of a vulture) drew back hastily, but not cravenly, from my hampered advance.

"Have a care, sir," warned the mate. "This is a desperate young devil!"

I could see that he to whom I had appealed possessed that cool caution which sometimes shares a man's character with physical timidity. He held himself out of reach of my free arm, but he held his common-sense as well.

"Thee need be in no such haste," says he to me— and even at that crisis, I noted how he used the uncouth English of the Quakers, yet spoke with the air of one accustomed to command. "This is a civilized commonwealth, and His Majesty's flag flies over it; thee is not to be hanged instanter, be thee what thee may. Thee shall have thy day in court."

"He robbed Captain Warcut," roared the mate, "and he has got the stolen money on him now!"

As he spoke thus, Grimshaw's left hand began to feel me for my little treasure.

Any number of days in court would have seemed of small use to me then. Grimshaw was a person of some maritime position; I was accounted a dangerous nobody, and the immigrants, too cowed to tell the truth and disavow my plotting mutiny, were nobodies, too. Doubtless, should it have come to a judge and jury, I would have won my freedom by disclosure of my relative's standing in the Province, yet you are to remember I was quite the mere boy that the Pimpled Man had called me: I knew nothing of law, but I knew the mate. I felt his groping fingers and so thought only robbery and death ahead of me, unless I wrung some juice of justice from this dry creature in rusty brown.

"I can prove my ownership and my respectability," I declared. "My uncle knows that this money is mine, and he must be known to some of you. He expects me; he is waiting for me. He is Master Simon Scull, Ranger of the Proprietor's Manor for the District of the Lower Susquehanna."

I had hoped for some effect from my wild speech, yet I had no such expectations as what then and there resulted. Grimshaw, it is true, began with a derisive laugh of unbelief, but it cracked; it ceased in mid-progress, and his hands loosed me. The port-officers fell away and gaped at the Pimpled Man, and he so far forgot his fears as to bend his round shoulders again

toward me and poke his blotched face almost into
mine.

A moment I bore his gaze, a moment watched his
mouth that chewed unspoken thoughts. Then he drew
me out of the group and walked me up the deck to that
spot where the Stranger and I had endured our siege.
Thereat he completed my amazement; he put a friendly
arm about me and, in a high, thin voice, says he:

" Nicholas, my name is Simon Scull."

Of course, you will say, I should have expected it,
and so, no doubt, I should.   Nevertheless, the plain fact
is that I did nothing of the sort.

In looking ahead, a boy's mind makes definite pictures and is slow to recognize the truth of things that
fall out otherwise. Thus, though for no reason in the
world, I had thought of my uncle not as coming aboard
ship, but as standing at the wharf to meet me when I
stepped ashore from a lighter. Again, if he was a
Quaker in the old days at home, I had no memory of
it, and finally, having forgotten his appearance and considering him in the part of an officer of the Province
and as my protector there, I had idealized him into a
noble figure. My wonder was great, but I counted
myself rescued from such dire peril that I could have
embraced a slave, were it one that liberated me. Ac-
cordingly, I wasted no time in speculation: I flung myself upon Uncle Simon and kissed his pimpled cheeks.

Somewhat embarrassed by my raptures, he released

himself, but he told me that he was glad to see me and glad to have been of early service.

" I had assumed," says he, " that thee would be below, collecting thy belongings, and I was about to inquire when all this violence occurred." His little eyes became yet smaller. " How is it," he asked, " that I find my nephew in such scandalous company? "

Straightway, I told him that the company was not scandalous. I declared that the Stranger was a very stranger to me, yet had saved my life. Like a rattling alarm-drum, I gave him my story.

He listened carefully, but without change of countenance. Then:

" So," he said, " Thomas Warcut and his mate would have treated thee as a mere creature of the Newlanders? "—Which was the term in those days for the emigration-agents in Europe, who were paid so much for each poor soul that they could persuade to embark for the Colonies, and would promise anything to earn their wage.—" How is it that thee did not tell them better? "

I was much distempered; I felt my face flame. " I blush," I asserted, " for my cowardice—not for my father."

I meant I was not ashamed of Lord Ravenscar, but that I had feared they would use me ill if they learned I was son of a crown-prisoner. Uncle Simon understood me and smiled wryly.

"Nor were thee, I hope, ashamed of me," he said by way of reprimand for what he took as my reluctance to announce to Warcut the standing of my American relative.

Then he turned to considering my present plight:

His influence, he said, was something, but his actual authority no vast matter in this corner of the Province. He could drop a word to-night to the justices in Philadelphia, so that there might perhaps be no difficulty with them in the morning; but a murder had been done —call the deed what I chose—and I had been on friendly terms with the murderer. Uncle Simon might get me safe away, once I was ashore, yet durst not hurry my landing, lest Grimshaw—a turbulent fellow and now in legal command of the boat—smell out the plan and spoil it by raising a popular clamor before it could be put into action. I must therefore remain aboard for the night—balking the mate's greed by confiding my money to my rescuer—and land next day, along with the other immigrants, when he would be on hand to smuggle me into the interior with the connivance of the law's own officers. There would not likely be any further trouble on the *John and Anne,* but if anything should fall amiss, I was to try to get word to him where he was lodged, at Andrew Bradford's, at the Sign of the Bible, in Second Street.

CHAPTER V

THE LORD PROPRIETOR

YOU can imagine with what reluctance I obeyed my uncle's instructions, yet obey them I did, for I had no choice, and, contrary to the admonitions of my pricking fears, no evil seemed to result. Simon Scull spoke aside to the mate—I was to suppose upon some official business—and presently went over the side with the port-officers. Grimshaw had not so much as a glance for me, and I huddled myself in the bow, close to the billet-head, where I passed the autumnal night in a wakefulness that proved reasonless. No molestation was attempted, and with the dawn all of us immigrants were hustled ashore and along the water-front much stared at and leered upon *en route,* but not once insulted until we were herded into the low-raftered common-room of what I was told was the Blue Anchor Tavern, at Dock Street and Front. Of Grimshaw we had not seen a sign.

There was no unfriendly air about the place, nor, indeed, much that was unfamiliar. The smells were those of rope and tar, and the apartment was clean. Somehow, these qualities suggested to me the idea that

40

my uncle's influence had been extended to all my ship-mates, and that we were to be permitted entrance to the Province without excess payment and on the original terms made in Europe by the Newlanders. The room was already half full of men whose plain dress and restrained bearing marked them as Quaker planters from the interior, and they seemed not at all of a sort to buy human folk into slavery. Still, I had scant opportunity to observe what befell, for, from among them, edged my stooping relative, who presently plucked at my sleeve.

"Come—come!" he whispered; "and quietly!"— as I made effusively to welcome him.

He bore himself with what I can describe only as a sort of Quaker swagger, and led me into a booth (one of many along those walls) having a table in it and high seats, like church-pews, on either side.

"I have managed with some success," says he, when we were seated; "but we had best be clear of this neigh-borhood ere your Master Grimshaw discovers our pur-pose. Your landing-money is short £2 of its total. I have gladly advanced that sum and require only a formal acknowledgment."

A strange greeting from uncle to nephew on the shores of the New World! It was so very strange that I could not then follow its implications.

"You mean ——" I began.

"Poof, lad! What's two pounds in the family?"

says my uncle. " 'Tis all a question of hurry now, lest Grimshaw interrupt."

That reference to the mate so frightened me as to leave me nothing else to think about, and it appeared that Uncle Simon shared my apprehension. He was manifestly eager for quickness. His long hands shook as he drew a parchment from his brown jacket that I did observe to bulge greatly for so lean a man, and remembered this peculiarity from yesterday; but of the parchment I noted only that it was well covered with writing in a clerkly hand.

" Sign here," says he, and puts a finger at the end of it.

There was an inkhorn and quill on the table, and I signed.

So did Uncle Simon, who next leaned around the corner of our booth and summoned two planters, and they witnessed the signatures. They were tall, tight-lipped persons wearing shovel-hats.

" Thee has begun the day's work early, Friend Simon," said one of them.

" Ever an early bird is Simon," smiled the second.

My uncle patted my shoulder. " And I have the worm—eh, nephew? " he asked.

Immediately he dismissed them and drew me along the crowd's edges to the open door. Some small delay there was there from the coming-in of other planters, and I paused, fronting a placard wafered to the panels.

Slowly I deciphered it without comprehending its import, as one will do such things when the body is forced to an unwilling pause while the mind is occupied with pressing terrors. I was searching the crowd for Grimshaw, so that, though the printed words slid into my brain, they left no impress on its surface.

"Hurry!" says my uncle, spying a chance of egress, and he pushed me into the street.

Once that we were clear of the tavern, his nervousness in part subsided, or at least expressed itself in a new manner. He kept a grip of my arm, but from brevity waxed loquacious, so that I found it well-nigh impossible, as folk say, to get in a word edgewise. His thin lips in a perpetual·smile, he maintained a running fire of talk, now pointing out this or that building of interest, and again discoursing on the glories of his estate near Hempfield, whither we were within the hour to be bound.

There was a change, too, in me. I, who had never left my own countryside until I left it for the port of departure, was in a strange land among a strange people, and it is small wonder if this conversation diverted me from reflections upon what had just passed at the Blue Anchor. I was all agape with the picture of so many houses so close together and so many people every one in a hurry and each centered on his own affairs moving restlessly between the rows of them. Gradually, the awe of Grimshaw itself thinned to a shade in the glare of my admiration for the sights of the city.

"Aye, Philadelphia is a bonny town," Uncle Simon said, in reply to my wide eyes, as, having climbed a hill, we set out along a bustling street extending westward; "but thee is to remember, lad, that we are going to another bonny place, though a lonely. 'Tis eighty mile of wilderness-road that we must travel, and that should be an experience for a lad of mettle."

I would have asked him somewhat of its dangers—of Indians, which bulked largest in my imagination, and of those apparently brigandish "Cresap's Men," of whom I had heard inquiry made by the crew to the port-authorities, aboard the *John and Anne*—but Uncle Simon went on with a smile that reminded me of something smooth and sweetish:

"Eighty-odd mile, and in a Conestoga wagon that's a house on wheels, Nicky. It'll be waiting us now in the square at t' town's end." There was a touch of the Yorkshire twang to his speech, and it warmed my heart because it echoed of home. "My servants will be ready," he said: "they had their orders early. And my steward with them, lad: Little Jacob, a gentle fellow, married to a good wife as will see to a boy's comfort with a kindlier eye than this of a simple-living, hard-working old bachelor."

All that he said I do not remember, but we came abreast of a red-brick building then, he mentioned,

44

newly completed, and lacking the steeple that you may see on it to-day. It was the place in which, not forty years later, our glorious Declaration of Independence was to be adopted.

As we passed by on the other side, a gentleman descended at the front of this building from a conspicuous coach. I made out that he was at once partially surrounded by retainers and had the bearing of importance; but Uncle Simon detecting him, as I thought, out of the corner of his eye took a tighter hold of my arm and noticeably increased our pace.

A voice sounded authoritatively from across the way: " Friend Simon! "

The tone was that of a man having power, yet not so deep in love with his dignity as to scorn to shout in a public thoroughfare. His call was clear, and passers-by turned to look from the speaker to us; but my conductor seemed not to hear it.

" Uncle," says I, " the gentleman over there is signalling you."

" Eh? " grunted my uncle and dragged me on.

I repeated my statement.

Uncle Simon did not raise his head. His air was not that of fear, but rather of preoccupation. In that manner of his, he chewed on nothingness and then:

" A mistake," he mumbled.

But we had not gone six paces before one of the retainers came running to us. He said something that, in my flurry, missed me, which nevertheless greatly altered my uncle: he stopped, became hugely apologetic—we crossed the street.   Arrived, he made to push me behind him and grew into a statue of respectfulness.

I moved somewhat to one side and had a moment's fair view of our summoner.   I observed that his clothes, while cut and colored like those of most of the other sober citizens whom we had passed on our walk, were yet of a finer quality and worn with a nicety far from provincial.

Uncle Simon was talking at even a greater rate than he had talked to me.   I gathered that he expressed himself as counting the meeting fortunate, in that he had fresh complaint to make of the mysterious and terrible " Cresap's Men," of whom, it seemed, I was never to hear the last.   Their unimpeded evil-doings fell in a waterfall from the Ranger's lips: their burning of farmsteads, their robbing of houses and their invariable escape from all pursuit.

It must have been with increasing impatience that the authoritative gentleman listened.   It was crisply that he interrupted:

" These affairs and those of all the Marylanders would sooner be settled if our Rangers did their full duty and if, when they planned counter-raids and arrests, they forebore to communicate their every scheme to loose fellows of looser tongues, who straightway bear this advance-news to the enemy."

THE LORD PROPRIETOR

Uncle Simon was attempting some excuse when my gaze travelled up to the gentleman's face. Here was a man in a wig meticulously curled; his cheeks owned none of the ruddiness of the colonist, the features so regular as to seem, at first glimpse, wanting in strength of character; the next, and it would be guessed that their owner's repose was not lethargic, but due rather to a perfection of self-mastery. I had got so far when his pale eyes which were somehow piercing, too, encountered mine and drove them into embarrassed retreat.

He divided again the cataract of my uncle's talk: "Who is this comely lad with thee?"

I think that Uncle Simon would gladly have escaped the answer to this inquiry. I know he made an endeavor to finish the sentence upon which he had been embarked, but the gentleman raised a hand white and well cared for, and I was dragged forward by my deprecating relative. I heard something that he said about his "dear nephew," but much of it was swallowed up in my wonderment when one term of address brought me to the realization that I was being presented to Thomas, son of the late William Penn, who, with his brother John—now long in England—was nothing less, if you please, than Proprietary of the Province of Pennsylvania.

I blushed furiously, thinking of my sea-stained clothes. Not knowing whether one should kiss the hand of a Lord Proprietor or merely bow, I did precisely nothing, and then, as I felt those pale eyes on my hanging head, Uncle Simon concluded:

" He is the son of my ill-disposed and unfortunate stepbrother, Francis, lately Earl of Ravenscar."

The Proprietary took my hand quite simply and bade me welcome to America. Even my confusion was no proof against his benignity, and to this you may be sure he increased my esteem of him, when I, feeling that Uncle Simon's speech had somewhat slighted my father, heard Thomas Penn saying to his Ranger:

" Thy stepbrother was worldly, Friend, nor was his cause mine, but I knew him, nor ever knew a braver gentleman; and, seeing what came to thee through his downfall, it ill becomes thee to speak lightly of him, in especial before his only child."

Thereat I could indeed have kissed this Quaker's hand; but Penn, as if surmising my boyish purpose, withdrew a step, and says he:

" Enough now, my lad. I called thy uncle merely that I might see thee: there were rumors concerning thy arrival, which rumors I shall put end to. Remember only this: if ever thee need help, send a message straight to me."

" Help? " echoes my uncle, quite recovering his ease or ever I could find an answer. " It was my affection brought him here, and 'tis my fatherly care will keep him."

Penn's face gave no token of how he received this. He signalled an end of the interview.

"That is as it should be, Friend Simon," he said. "See to it that the boy comes to no harm."

Thus were we dismissed; and why I then knew not, but as we resumed our progress up the street, there emerged to the surface of my brain a clear picture of that placard which I had read at the water-front tavern. I saw it again before me, dated, early though the hour had been, that very morning, and now I understood at least its significance for my fellow-immigrants:

> Yesterday arrived from Rotterdam and Plymouth, in the ship *John and Anne*, Thos. Warcut, Master, a parcel of likely servants on board the said ship, to be sold reasonable for money or country-produce; credit given if required.

So, after all, my poor shipmates were to suffer from the dead Warcut's unconscionable advance of the passage-price! Those who could not pay it were to be made slaves. Few, I knew, had the additional capital—none, save myself, would find here a generous relative to lend him what he so desperately required. I could have wept for their straits, and I thanked God for my odd uncle, who had rescued me. It was little I divined how heavily my own future would be affected by that placard of the Blue Anchor.

CHAPTER VI

THE WILDERNESS ROAD

SUCH, so close as recollection serves, was the state of my mind when we left the Lord Proprietor's presence. You may ask whether I gave any thought to other facts about my uncle.

Acquainted with the arbitrary nature of the raising of the passage-cost, why had he, an officer of the Province, entered no protest against it, but permitted the sale of the immigrants to go on? Well, I may have been selfish enough to excuse him as avoiding public appearance in order to protect me from Grimshaw. The same apology might serve his endeavor to avoid Mr. Penn. But how was I, so loyal to my father, to palliate deprecating mention of that parent when there had been no need to speak of him at all?

I simply do not remember what I then thought of these matters, and this because they were soon swallowed up in another. What that was you are now to hear.

When we reached the square whither we had been bound, it was full of those hulking covered-wagons wherein the planters haul their produce and often their families along the Wilderness Road to Philadelphia.

Near the pavement, making ready for departure, was my uncle's own cavalcade in a violent convulsion.

A very giant of a man, whose skin shone like copper above the bulging muscles of his bared arms, had seized two smaller fellows of similar color. He held one with either fist and was literally knocking their heads together. The sound of it was like axe-blows on a tree-trunk, and the poor wretches' cries had attracted a crowd of other wagoneers, who heartlessly looked on with no comment save laughter.

Although I had never seen Indians before, I yet realized that this tormentor and his captives alike belonged to that race. My first sensation was of disappointment, for I had pictured redmen as always going about with feathered head-dresses and paint-streaked cheeks, whereas these specimens were clad like Europeans, so far as they had any clothes at all. Nevertheless, the sight of the big one was grisly enough to suit my fancy of a savage, and something that soon came over his grisliness was still more terrible.

He stood quite six-feet-six and was broad according. His black hair was a matted jungle, his face a mass of scars and bulges. What was worse, it was clear even to me that this savage did not feel so much anger at his victims as delight in the suffering he inflicted on them, and this he showed in a horrible manner. With every concussion of their heads, he opened his mouth in a wide grin, revealing fangs and stumps yellow and

black, and he raised his head so as to disclose his eyes:
the right gleamed with delirious pleasure; the left, white
and sightless, rolled loosely in its socket.

" Jacob—Little Jacob! "

It was Uncle Simon speaking. He spoke so low that
I wondered how his words could carry through the
noise of this fracas, but their effect was instantaneous
and powerful.

The Susquehannock—for to that fierce tribe my
uncle's steward belonged—dropped the pair of peaceable Shawanese to the ground, who crawled whimper-
ing to the wagon. Jacob's legs smote together; his face
grew livid under its copper; his jaw fell. The blind
eye threatened to roll away, and the good one closed
itself as if too abjectly afraid to meet the gaze of his
master. Fearsome as he had been, there was that which
was more shocking in this spectacle of such ruthlessness
reduced to abject panic at the unexpected appearance
of a stoop-shouldered weakling whom he could have
broken across his knee.

I looked for the cause. There was nothing changed
in Uncle Simon. His pimpled face showed not even
annoyance; his red-rimmed eyes merely twinkled, and
over his lips spread only a reproving smile. He shook
his finger as if at a querulous child.

" Jacob," said he, " this will not do."

The giant flung himself on his knees. He mumbled
that the other Indians had protested against further

work, because they had been all night busy to make ready for our journey. He crouched and cringed and grovelled, so that I drew away in an unexplainable repugnance.

" Get up," said Uncle Simon, " and hasten our start. " I shall not interfere with discipline."

The steward's gratitude promised to be more sickening than his pleas, but this was cut short. My uncle, spinning 'round on his heel, sent him through the already dwindling crowd, to our wagon.

" Poor Little Jacob," my uncle said, " is usually more circumspect, but when he drinks too deep of what he calls ' fire-water,' he is somewhat rough-handed."

I will not seek to tell you of my private feelings on this topic, nor yet impose on you a description of our departure and the country we subsequently traversed. The land is not so greatly altered in this Year of Grace 1781, but that you may still see much the same wooded rolling country on your own journeys through it, though you are to remember that it was then even more sparsely settled than now, and that we had not long left the town ere we were following a track on either side of which stretched miles and miles untenanted by any white man. Our progress, moreover, was greatly similar to that which you would make to-day: one Shawanese, Iron Hatchet, drove the wagon; the other, called Billy, had in charge several led-horses, and Uncle Simon and Little Jacob rode their own mounts, my relative being ungainly astride his favorite, a service-able white mare.

Two incidents of our leaving you should, however, keep in mind:

I felt so sorry for the maltreated Shawanese that I watched my chance and, while Uncle Simon and his steward were in conversation, I surreptitiously shook each of those unfortunates by the hand. Their grati-tude was moving and, later, bore fruit that served me well.

This was the first. The second was that, when my uncle and Little Jacob had finished their talk, the Sus-quehannock, with his fanged grin, pointed to a restless stallion, a splendid animal, plainly a thoroughbred, long, fully sixteen hands high, among the led-horses, and says he to me with the face of a basilisk:

" Master say Mr. Nicky heap brave boy. Mr. Nicky ride? "

Now, in my last year at home, I had become an ex-cellent horseman, for my age, and I immediately wanted to ride that stallion; yet something—not modesty, I am certain, but more like a repulsion to the steward's grin —made me answer only:

" I ride a little."

" This heap fine horse," said Little Jacob. " If Mr. Nicky brave boy, him ought ride like big man."

Nowadays it seems always to me an evil portent when a savage smiles, but then I knew nothing of redmen or

their minds: all that appeared to me from the Susquehannock's tone was what we boys used to call a
"dare," and that I was never a lad to suffer. The
animal looked very fresh, but I believed that I could
manage him and meant, anyhow, to try.

"He is ready saddled," said I: "cut him out and
bring him here."

Uncle Simon intervened. "No, no," he ordered,
looking at vacancy. "We shall wait till we are beyond
the city and the way is clear."

So, at a sign from him, I perforce clambered on to
the driver's seat of the Conestoga-wagon, beside Iron
Hatchet, and, as I have said, our party left Philadelphia and swung at last into "the Wilderness Road."
There little by little, yet steadily withal the woods closed
on either hand; chestnut, oak and pine crowded the
wayside, the two former varieties in an autumnal glory
of yellow and red, and the ground beneath them was
thick with a jungle of burr-bearing bushes. As far
ahead as I could see, and as far back, there was nothing
but this and the highway. We were more alone than I
had ever been before. One spot was exactly like another, so that I could never after, in retravelling that
route, determine where there happened what now befell, but this, when we were well forth of the city, was
the manner of it:

I had been speaking with my uncle of the weather,
and he saying that this season was what the colonists

called their "Indian Summer," corresponding to our St. Martin's Summer at home, and that it was like to end in a fierce thunder-storm, one day or another, and then turn of a sudden to dead cold, with frost, or even snow, when abruptly says he, and I wondered how he guessed the strength of my resolve:

"If thee has really made up thy mind to attempt the stallion, nephew, why this bit of road is as likely a place for that experiment as any."

He nodded to the Susquehannock, who dismounted and lashed his own horse to a tree. A quick disquietude struck me, and I watched him well, yet all that I saw was that he stooped once among the bushes. Then he released the stallion from among the animals in Billy's keeping and brought him toward me.

"Shorten the stirrups," said Uncle Simon, with a strange alteration of his voice.

He was obeyed. The stallion seemed to resent this, or else he was wilder when unled, for he reared and whinnied. Little Jacob leered in my direction.

"Too good horse for any boy-afraid," he chuckled; and his blind eye rolled and seemed to laugh blindly.

But I was not afraid, and the insinuation more than ever determined me. I made a clean vault into the saddle.

No sooner did my weight descend than the stallion went to his knees, uttering a cry like a human creature in pain, and at once rebounded with a shriek of pure rage. That was the beginning.

I dug my knees tight for dear life. I twisted the reins about my wrist and tossed my body back so as to throw all my weight upon the bit.—I was not the twinkling of an eye too soon.

You would have thought that I had mounted a cyclone. Snorting, even yelping, the mad beast lashed himself into a perfect paroxysm of anger. He curvetted and whirled like a dancing dervish; he turned and tried to snap at me. He catapulted to one side of the road and bashed himself against the trees so that I thought my leg had broken, as he meant it should; then he shot to the other side and repeated the manœuvre there. Sweat poured from him in rivulets, foam came on his flanks as if from an unheard-of snowfall. He shook himself and me: my teeth beat one upon another with a noise that, had it been audible above his own yells and the crash of his insane hoofs, must have resembled the clatter of a watchman's rattle sounding an alarm.

He arched his back so as to flip me upward from the saddle, then swerved as I came down until, a dozen times, in stranglingly sudden succession, I all but lost my seat; he reared high on his hind legs, pawing the air above my head and threatening a sheer backward fall that must have been instantly fatal.

How I remained astride him I know not. I so plied

my heels that I thought his ribs had burst: I might as well have kicked a stone-wall. I sawed at his mouth till blood flecked the froth on it: he felt it no more than if the bit had been straw. He tried every murderous trick again and again, with an infinite variety in the order; he sometimes seemed to try them all at once, and this with the quickness of lightning, so that there was no second to realize our struggle before I was engaged in another of diverse character, demanding an altogether different balance and resistance. I have said that I was a fair horseman, but this was beyond the bounds of nature: only the favor of Heaven kept me mounted and alive.

I knew it and now, not knowing when it would desert me, I was indeed afraid. I understood that my very existence was at stake, and that to let go the reins and try to leap to the road would only precipitate my end. I looked into the wide mouth of terror, and yet at the very centre of my battle I was strangely aware, through the billowy dust-cloud that enveloped me, of an extraneous condition:

The caravan had come to pause. Iron Hatchet, from his wagon-seat, and Billy from his saddle, were looking at me with eyes as large as half-crown pieces. My uncle, reining-in the white mare, stooped forward and peered at the mêlée with cheeks that seemed to have been dipped in flour; but Little Jacob, quieting his own horse by a careless hand, was watching my fight with a countenance of mixed malevolence and glee that I shall never forget.

One thought, and one alone, burst into full blaze— as it were the sun rising at midnight—on the darkness of my mind. The reason of it I guessed not, but the fact was Gospel-revelation:

" Here, by this Indian's hand, is foul play! "

I strove to call out to my uncle: how could he have heard me? Rather it was as if, unable to help, he could not bear further sight of my struggles. My stallion reared more desperately than ever; Uncle Simon thrust a hand before his eyes and then clapped spurs to his mare and, bending far over her neck, bolted west along the Wilderness Road.

Well, so much of what I saw my crazy beast must also have seen, and it was the last whip to his dementia. His forefeet thundered to the roadway. In a gallop that snatched the breath from my throat, he sped after the runaways.

After them? I had better say *at* them! He pounced abreast and flung himself and me against them as he had flung me against the tree-trunks.

At once Uncle Simon and I were unhorsed and lying in the highroad together—and Uncle Simon was lying very still.

CHAPTER VII

BIVOUAC

NOT half a minute could have passed before I staggered to my feet, with the world spinning 'round me, for we had gone no great distance, and yet a glance down the see-sawing road revealed the three Indians not yet started after us.

I leaned above Uncle Simon. Was he dead?

To determine whether his heart still beat, I ripped open his brown jacket and the not overly-clean shirt beneath it. His heart was beating; it beat above an oddly lumpy money-belt that was buckled close around his body, next the skin.

I thought that all constrictions should be removed and started to loosen this one, but I had some difficulty with the clasp. I was fumbling hotly when there came running feet behind.

" You keep hand off! "

Little Jacob's steel claws gripped my collar. The Susquehannock pitched me roughly into the road.

My first idea was that he now meant to murder us both, but of this I was disabused. He worked with forest-skill, and a certain gentleness, upon my uncle, who was shortly upright, supported by his steward's

arm. I decided that, whatever the cause of Little
Jacob's hatred, it was directed against me alone, and
that I must seek an opportunity secretly to acquaint
Uncle Simon of it, who, opening his red-rimmed eyes,
smiled wanly at me now. But, says he, bravely enough,
though in a tremulous voice:

"Nephew, a word with thee." And when I drew
nearer, under the Susquehannock's very glare: "I con-
gratulate thee on thy horsemanship," says my uncle.

Little Jacob would not leave him. I therefore mur-
mured some confused thanks and begged my relative
—at the same time inquiring of his hurts—to forgive
the collision. He had not impressed me as a courageous
man, yet he made light of both my topics. He was but
a little bruised, he said, and would remount so soon as
Billy brought him back his mare. As for me, I had been
marvellous, and he would never excuse himself for let-
ting me have my way and mounting me on a newly
bought horse.

"Why, there the impudent fellow is," says he in his
high, thin voice, nodding westward, "as quietly munch-
ing leaves as if he were a palfrey! Jacob, we must have
him shot!"

I saw the stallion, engaged as my uncle said, a little
way beyond us, and so fine an animal he was that I
pleaded for him. His owner was loath to pardon.

"But he will be better now," said I: "I know that
he will be better now!"

I was none too sure just then, but a moment more confirmed me. I ran alone to the stallion, who saw me, moved off a trifle and might have bolted but that I was too quick for him. The saddle had slipped; I began to straighten it—and there, beneath the saddle-cloth, was a handful of burrs that had, of course, cut into the beast the moment I bestrode him.

I remembered how Little Jacob had stooped among the bushes before shortening the stirrups, but it would be bad policy to let him see what I guessed. Placing myself between the horse and the onlookers, I removed the cause of the trouble. The stallion seemed to understand; he turned on me eyes that, I could swear, were eyes of gratitude. The wound was not so deep as, with the burrs gone, to make a rider painful to him; I sprang into the saddle: the splendid animal was like a lamb, and I may add that, though he would not tolerate any other master, he was from that moment my devoted slave.

I could fancy that Little Jacob thought a thing or two, and that he was no ways pleased with the immediate turn of events, but the rest of our party were seemingly frank in the expression of their sentiments. That mercy of Providence which had kept me so long on the struggling animal's back and later subdued him altogether, the Shawanese regarded as a miracle wrought by myself and were almost ready to worship me for it, and Uncle Simon was equally lost in wonder and admiration.

So we rode on, and ever deeper into the wilderness. Clearings became rarer; at about high noon, we passed one caravan, rather like our own, but travelling in the contrary direction, yet from that hour until sunset our way was entirely lonely. Except for the road itself, I might have thought us explorers of a virgin continent.

All this while, Little Jacob gave me never a chance to speak with my uncle in private. The giant, of the cruelty of whose nature I had received so many and such startling proofs, professed a tender concern for the possible effects upon Uncle Simon of his fall; he uttered not one syllable about my own, but he followed the Ranger like his shadow, and from time to time suggested rests, offered comforts and, in short, would not let us be. It was not until nightfall that I got my opportunity.

Then we reached a clearing, but a natural one, by the roadside, without sight of any cabin or ever hint of man; and here, it appeared, we were to bivouac. The wagon was drawn from the highway and through a clump of beach-trees; Billy picketed the horses, except my stallion, which would have nobody near him save me and even bit at Little Jacob in passing, and Iron Hatchet made a fire and began to cook our supper.

I confess that, for a brief period, my fears weakened. A great peace wrapped us 'round. The night was full of stars; there was no wind, yet some breath must have stirred the neighboring trees, for they whispered comfort, and, as I was a tired and healthy boy, the smell of Iron Hatchet's frying bacon was so homely and so full of the promise of physical satisfaction that I began to ask myself whether I had not exaggerated the dangers of my plight.

Immediately we had eaten—a ceremony that might not begin until Uncle Simon had said grace—he and I climbed into the Conestoga-wagon, where beds, by no means rude, had been prepared for us. He explained that the Indians would sleep and watch outside, turn and turn about.

The wagon was large, and, peeping beneath its canvas, I saw that we were at last out of earshot of our companions. The Shawanese had already rolled themselves in blankets; with their heads to the flickering fire, they lay as still as logs placed there to feed the embers ere the morning. Just at the edge of the darkness, and with no more sound than would have been made by a shadow, the giant Susquehannock paced the circle of our camp, a ready rifle in the crook of his arm: as head-servant, he had chosen the first and easiest watch.

If I were that night to communicate my suspicions to my uncle, it seemed that it had best be now. I turned to him. The fire outside pushed a half-light through the canvas, and I noted that he was just rising from his knees.

BIVOUAC

"Uncle," said I, "I saw something this morning about which I must tell you."

He was at once upright and fronting me.

"Eh?" said he. "Saw something? What?"

You might imagine that this anxiety would increase my own: it did not. Rather, as I sought words to tell my tale, those which I found all seemed pale and unconvincing. I think I would then have drawn back from my project, but he had gripped my shoulders, and his hands were shaking and peremptory. Scarce, somehow, could I hide a shudder at his touch.

"What did thee see?" he asked. And again: "What?"

It was as if he shook the thing from me. It fell out of my mouth in a single sentence childishly formed:

"Somebody had put burrs under my stallion's saddle, and that was what made him behave as he did, and it was Little Jacob did it—and, Uncle, I think he meant to kill me!"

Uncle Simon loosed his hold. His face was hid by the shade of one of the hoops that supported the canvas wagon-top, but I heard him laugh and the cackle of it was all one of relief.

"So he played thee that old trick!" cried my uncle. "It is rude and it is dangerous; it was very wrong of him to play it upon his master's nephew, but it is a common one in these parts; they use it on most new-comers, and it is not ill-intended."

I might doubt the intention, but how near ill the effects were he himself had seen. Shamed by his ridicule, I stubbornly pointed out to him the narrowness of his escape and mine.

That had small effect. He declared again that what I had undergone was, as I revealed it, a species of initiation and an example of frontier humor. It would be unwise to stir up trouble while we travelled; on our reaching Hempfield, Little Jacob should be mildly punished for daring to joke with a person of my position —especially as, in the case of one so young, it might have resulted seriously—but I was really only taking offense at a joke that came sooner or later to every pioneer.

I blushed, I think, as he proceeded, and I was glad that the light was insufficient to betray me. I did not like the Susquehannock better than before, but I did not any longer suspect him of more than wanton cruelty, and so I was relieved when my uncle's tone changed again to one of anxiety and he resumed his hold of my arm:

" So that was all thee saw? That was all? Nothing that seemed strange to thee? "

" Why, yes," said I. " What else was there? "

" I speak," he insisted, " about the whole affair. Thee was first to come to me when I had fallen. For that I thank thee.—Yet this was all that thee saw? "

He puzzled me now, and so I said. Thereat he

sighed, and released me, his sigh sounding the same relief that his chuckle had lately done.

"Of course not," said he, "for there was nothing more to be seen. It is merely that folk think I carry valuables, and thee, who opened my shirt, as Little Jacob tells me—thee saw a money-belt, which—between us, nephew—holds naught but some papers relating to the government of the Province."

I told him I should not have remembered the belt had he not recalled it.

"Just so," says he, "but there are others less honest. Thee sees that we set sentries? People might think that was done against robbers: it is only against possibly unfriendly redmen. The Indian, Nicky, is not bettered by better conditions. As a savage, he has at least the savage's pride; as a half-civilized being, he becomes a broom-maker and a basket-maker in name, and a beggar and a thief in fact. In my travels, I am careful never to carry anything valuable about me. Should ever any man ask thee questions, remember that, nephew: nothing of value—oh, never anything of value at all!"

CHAPTER VIII

THE QUAKER MAGISTRATE

NOT much happened to beguile our journey until it was well-nigh half complete. The country continued lonely; we encountered but two or three other parties of travellers, and these all headed east, nor, though our progress was not rapid, did we stay for any traffic with them. Little Jacob, indeed, once discovered some means of intoxication, which displayed itself in his evilly beating Iron Hatchet and the wagon's horses with their driver's rawhide, and in deepening my dislike of him; but Uncle Simon brought him to his senses by a smooth admonition, and the Susquehannock (who patently both feared and loved his master) straightway grovelled as he had done in the square at Philadelphia. Yet this action on the part of my relative—if anything so quiet deserves the name of action—was his sole demonstration of authority: generally, he swayed carelessly along astride his white mare, his thin shanks dangling, the bridle half the time free from his forgetful fingers; he spoke seldom and gave every appearance of a man brooding over distant affairs.

Having circled the sources of Darby Creek—all

decked-out in their gay autumn-livery—we passed, as you must be aware, between highlands and entered the wide valley, bordered by imposing hills, that takes name from the County of Chester. So we reached the right branch of the Brandywine and came to the village of Milltown distributed over rising ground on both sides of this stream.

Here my uncle was for making no stay, but we met several persons to whom he was known, and one of these —I think he was the owner of the mill—coming in face of us on the highroad and being a person of consequence, could not be slighted. It happened that I rode then close behind Uncle Simon and heard all that passed. The conversation was of no importance, save for one reference, but that reference I record:

The mill-owner, having made his greetings and cast an inquiring gaze at me—to which my uncle paid no heed—asked the news of Philadelphia. When that was given in terms so brief as to brush the wall dividing common politeness from discourtesy, he continued:

"We have had no news of further disturbances from Cresap's men."

Uncle Simon grunted.

"Nevertheless," continued the mill-owner, who was evidently familiar with the Ranger's strange habits of speech, "I could wish that we had some assurance of better help from the authorities. Did you see the Lord Proprietor in the city?"

" Aye," says my uncle.

" And did you lay before him your complaint of too little assistance? "

Uncle Simon's red-rimmed eyes showed plainly his resentment at this interference with his duty.

" I did," said he, " but I may tell thee nothing more of't than this: that t'Lord Proprietor made no promises."

Still the questioner persisted:

" This is a strange matter! Are we never, then, to have any guarantes of safety? "

The Ranger's temper was not proof against that. " What more can I do than I have done, without armed and organized assistance? " he demanded.

" But," stammered the mill-owner, " you do not take my intention. I am not impugning *your* courage or diligence ——"

" Then take thy complaints to Philadelphia where thee thinks t'fault lies," Uncle Simon tossed at him and, without any farewell, he rode away.

Of necessity I followed, and, when we had gone some little distance, I made bold to ask a question on my own part concerning this Cresap and his adventures.

" Thee had best hold thy tongue," he snapped at me, and then he added: " If I am no better supported than I of late have been, belike we shall all learn more of these rebels to our sorrow."

THE QUAKER MAGISTRATE

After this rebuff, as you may fancy, I hesitated about again addressing him.

The farther we proceeded from Milltown, the wilder grew the district through which we passed. The few farmsteads gave place to log-cabins, more widely scattered, and these became less and less frequent, the ultimate signs of civilization being a friendless grist-mill or a solitary tavern, separated from all other tokens of human existence.

A sense of isolation descended on me like a fog. It was scarce relieved by Billy's advice, given on the afternoon of our fourth day, that we now ride with greater slowness in order to arrive at our destination as fresh as might be: the knowledge that we neared our journey's end was no comfort when it promised residence in an almost uninhabited wilderness. You may understand, then, my joy when, tardily as we went, we unexpectedly overtook even a single horseman riding in our own direction.

We came upon him after a sharp turn in the road, without warning, or, I am convinced, Uncle Simon would have stopped to let him keep his lead of us. Certain it is that I heard the Ranger mutter an expression of disgust when the encounter revealed itself as inevitable; then, as the man thus overhauled turned and bowed with dignified gravity, my uncle broke into profuse salutations. You would have thought he wanted nothing but this encounter to complete his earthly hap-

71

piness, and he made that kind of flattering to-do over its object that I have often seen made by a female of modest station over some high-placed lady whom, until the lady condescended to her, she has been pretending to despise.

I was beside Billy, at the head of the led-horses. "Who," I whispered, "is this gentleman?"

"Him live near us," grunted the Shawanese, in evident liking. "Him Crown Magistrate. Him John Wright."

I had now full view of this officer, who was dressed in Quaker garb, the cloth of excellent quality, and rode these dangerous paths, as I observed, unarmed. From under his wide-brimmed hat, thin red hair fell to his neckcloth, but there was gathered in a sort of nautical pigtail and secured by a knot of black ribbon. He was clean-shaven, his nose straight, his mouth firm, and his almost black eyes were deeper set in the head than any I had ever beheld. A stern man, I should have thought, but just and fearless, and I could not but observe that he was none too pleased with Uncle Simon.

He had me brought to him and was decently civil. My uncle made much of me in his presence, but soon nodded an order that I fall behind. Of what was then talked about I have no information, yet surmised that, whereas it was the Ranger who sought to conceal his feelings, neither man felt partiality to the other's company, and that they continued together because there was one only road, and separation without rudeness proved impossible.

The sun set; the twilight descended. Because of our nearness to our destination, we were not to pause for that. The shadows of the trees pressed closer around us; but a full moon nosed red above the encompassing pines, and, in an atmosphere of lunar rose, we still progressed toward Lancaster.

Little Jacob had dropped to the rear. The Shawanese were silent. The voices of Mr. Wright and Uncle Simon seemed lowered in respect to the death of day, and I, from thinking of my big, laughing father far away and a royal prisoner, of a sudden fell afraid. Risking my elders' displeasure, I pushed my stallion close behind the animals on which they were mounted.

This was our situation when, with a mighty tearing of the bushes, a man on horseback broke from the woods immediately before us and, drawing his own reins, brought us also to a breathless stop.

" Halt! " he cried, and I saw a levelled pistol in his extended right hand.

He was cloaked—jack-booted—masked. I had heard at home enough gossip of the Great North Road to understand that here was a highwayman.

CHAPTER IX

THE HIGHWAYMAN

WHAT I understood, the others understood also and even, I take it, the horses. Those abruptly checked beasts reared high with snortings and a clatter of hind hoofs. Uncle Simon's turned completely and whirled him back of me. The Shawanese must have been terrified out of all resistance and were of no protective value. In the rear, I heard a confused clatter as of one horse going and another galloping up: Little Jacob's animal flew into the midst of us, scattering us to either side of the road, the giant Susquehannock, a savage drunk with battle, heading him straight for the brigand.

Nor is it to be supposed that the masked man was meanwhile inactive. His movements, indeed, were the very perfection of precise celerity. His free hand twitched his bridle. Without an inch to spare, he was safe and, as Little Jacob flashed by, the fist that held the pistol struck the steward out of the saddle.

I urged my stallion beside Mr. Wright, on the wild impulse of helping him: he made a gesture to restrain me. The highwayman's pistol was now again presented to us, but Mr. Wright remained unmoved.

74

THE HIGHWAYMAN

"Friend," he announced—and his voice was as calm as if he rebuked merely a saucy servant—"I would have thee note that I am unarmed, but I am a Crown-Officer, and I demand thy surrender."

Our enemy's reply was a shout of derisive laughter. He tossed his head upward; and, had the light been better, I might have seen at least the outline of his features, for the mask seemed to fit them like a glove and terminated above the mouth. As it was, however, all that I could distinguish was his parted lips, and from these his mirth rang carefree and loud.

"Why," says he, "that's an offer indeed; but I care little for your Crown at this time and not one jot for surrender at any." And at that he urged his horse quite abreast of my new companion and poked the barrel of his murderous weapon against Mr. Wright's chest. "So you are a dead man!" he shouted.

I thought then that it was all over. I averted my gaze and so looked where Little Jacob had fallen.

The Susquehannock, his blind eye rolling vindictively, was cautiously rising. His good eye glittered, and I could conjecture, since I could not well see, his black and yellow fangs uncovered by a grin. His rifle had rolled safe beyond recovery, but now a long knife shone in his fist. He caught me watching him spellbound and raised a warning finger: he had yet some yards to traverse before attacking the highwayman from behind, and it was clear that he wanted to surprise him.

Was there time? I glanced back at my companion: although that pistol was pressed against his heart, he was declaring that the " ruffian "—for so he boldly called him—committed a felony in resisting arrest!

" I am John Wright of Hempfield," he concluded, " and a King's Magistrate."

The effect of that name was magical. The masked man's pistol dropped to his side. He turned to me.

" Is this the truth? " he demanded.

Something choked my words, but I nodded.

The mask laughed again, yet now as if at some folly of his own. With a gesture the most romantical, he swept off his plumed hat.

I could scarce believe the living testimony of my eyes, but I was forced to credit what they next showed me, for I turned them on Little Jacob. He stood atiptoe behind this amazing marauder; his vast stature assured the blow, and the arm that held the bare knife crept upward.

Everything had altered now, and I wanted to cry out; but a very paralysis gripped me. I could not move; my lips were frozen. And through this nightmare-horror, the merry voice of the unguessing victim sounded:

" Mr. Magistrate," said the mask, " I salute a brave man, and that is always a pleasure. Pray mark: I have not required your money—though that is no great matter. I want it not, nor the person of any law-officer.

What I do want is Master Simon Scull, for he is the only mother's son worth my robbing betwixt the Susquehanna and the Schuylkill!"

Until then I had been too wrought upon to heed his voice and had got only the purport of his words. Now the tone of his speech struck against my consciousness and, rebounding, shattered the palsey of my throat.

My shriek directed Mr. Wright's glance, which had been glued to the highwayman, and he saw the Susquehannock in the act of assassination:

"Jacob, put down that knife!"

There was no calm in the Quaker now. The command came with the anger of a pistol-shot, and, as if it were a bullet that struck Little Jacob's hand, his blade clattered to the roadway.

The highwayman turned but a flash of his mask on Little Jacob, as that one slunk snarling among the shadows.

"Sir," said the rescued man to the Magistrate, "I thank you." He bent toward me: "And you, lad, also."

Mr. Wright appeared already ashamed of his outburst. "I will have no murder done," he grumbled—"not if it be to save my life. And now," he continued, "remember that thee is under arrest."

In the red moonlight, I saw the masked man smile.

"Mr. Magistrate," he answered, "your spirit is so much better than Master Runaway Scull's as almost to persuade my surrender. Moreover, I owe you and the boy here somewhat for this evening's work, so that, even as a ' ruffian,' happen I may yet be of service to you— but at the moment I may not accept your hospitality."

I think this first brought to us the realization of my uncle's flight and that it was his mare that had galloped to the rear when Little Jacob charged. But thereof we took no great account, for, while Mr. Wright was thus speaking, here was an immediate happening to stir us: no sooner had the masked man ceased speaking than his fingers regained the reins, and his spurs dug into his horse's flanks.

" Room, gentlemen! " he laughed. " Room, if you please! "

We fell aside like so many stupid serving-lads; and, before any could raise even a word of protest, he had dashed down the road and out of our vision in the direction which Uncle Simon had taken.

I hoped that this would result in no evil to my relative, but I vowed to hold my peace if it did not, for, when I had at last wakened to it, the voice of the masked man seemed familiar. His departure was an action worthy of my heroic Stranger of the *John and Anne*— and, unless my memory betrayed me, he *was* that stranger!

CHAPTER X

CRESAP'S MEN

I AM compelled to admit that none of my fellow-travellers exhibited any large distress at Uncle Simon's absence. Mr. Wright, though he made some pretense to regret the escape of the highwayman, yet declared the futility of pursuit and pulled down the corners of his mouth at thought of the Ranger's cowardice, while Little Jacob, endeavoring to conceal chagrin at being deprived of a murder, announced that his master's knowledge of every trail in this district would fully guarantee his safety. It was therefore decided that we should press forward.

And here it was that I first saw Mr. Wright at his best, for he bade me ride beside him, and the stern Magistrate disappeared, the severe Quaker vanished, and only a very considerate gentleman remained. He paid me, without parading the payment, that most palatable compliment which maturity can offer youth: he treated me as if I were of his own age. He in no way patronized me, yet contrived to speak highly of my composure during the attack—a laudation that I accepted guiltily, remembering my real distress of mind; he thanked me for my attempt to help him against the

79

brigand, which he said that he prevented because he would not see me come to harm " even in defence of the King's Highway."

Now I heard much of what was to be my new home: how the settlers worked and lived, most of them holding to their kind, but others—like one Martin Chartière and his son Peter, on Pequa Creek—marrying Indian squaws and becoming, to all intent, redmen themselves; how the Province paid bounties for the pelts of wolves and foxes, and a score of other matters tending to the same general purpose. In short, my newly-found friend made so very free with me—yet without any derogation to his own dignity—and so, by his confidence, raised me in my own esteem, that, as we went along, I soon felt secure to put to him the question my uncle had declined to answer.

" I have heard much," I said, " of persons called ' Cresap's Men.' What are they? "

And so he told me.

It is a long story, but, as you shall see, my fortunes, and therefore yours, were to be deeply concerned with it, and so you must bear with me while I tell it now. It shall be as briefly stated as it can be:

Lord Baltimore, the Proprietor of Maryland, said Mr. Wright, wishing to advance the northern boundary of his Colony up to and across the Susquehanna, had selected for his agent a pliant and bold adventurer, Thomas Cresap, and sent him to settle first in the Cone-

johela Valley and thereafter on an island called " The
Isle of Promise " in the river, both of which spots had
theretofore been considered a part of Pennsylvania.
Baltimore counted on the non-resistance of Penn's
Colonists, because they were largely folk whose religion
forbade fighting, so that this Cresap was originally intended to be no more than an opening wedge for a quiet
invasion of Maryland settlers, who should thus possess
the coveted land.   But men's severest principles are
weak before the seizure of their property: the non-
resisters resisted, whereupon Cresap assumed a more
violent offensive and was now become, with the secret
connivance of the Maryland authorities at Annapolis,
little better than a leader in guerilla warfare.

It was true that he exceeded Lord Baltimore's expressed desire, but the fact remained that this agent's
headquarters were a base to which armed Marylanders
resorted—much reinforced by runaway debtors and escaped criminals from our own Commonwealth—and
from which they conducted constant raids upon the surrounding territory.   Philadelphia was so far away that
the Pennsylvania Government, seated there, received
news of all this with too much philosophy and provided
its southern people almost no assistance; but pitched
battles were not infrequent, in which the invaders generally had the better of it, and houses were burned,
crops destroyed, live-stock carried off and occasional
Pennsylvanians kidnapped.

The narrative reminded me of those stories of Scotch border-warfare which had beguiled my earliest childhood.

" Very like," said Mr. Wright, with the first touch of his former severity, " but not to be admired for that reason."

He went on to tell me that the ringleader in these enterprises, though frequently heading the raids in person, had never yet been clearly enough observed to be legally identified in the unlikely event of his capture. It was known that he now maintained an almost inaccessible stronghold, called Cresap's Fort, among the forests on the farther side of the Susquehanna, and that he had another on the Isle of Promise, that wooded island, which could be reached by those alone who were familiar with the treacherous currents, and then only in shallow skiffs, so that attack-in-force was well-nigh impossible.

I felt that my sympathies should be with my adopted Colony.

" But," I therefore inquired, " are there not enough brave men in Pennsylvania somehow to overcome these difficulties? I should think 'twould be a simple matter to gather a force and drive them off."

The Magistrate smiled at my zest.

" Bravery well applied," he answered, " is an excellent quality, but there is here needed something more than courage. There is needed ingenuity, which we may possess, and discretion, in which we seem somewhat lacking."

He explained that there was a heavy reward for Cresap's capture, and that many attempts were launched to secure it, but that all failed. The most carefully devised plans seemed always to reach the outlaw's ears, so that whenever one of his hiding-places was approached at a time when its garrison was thought to be safely diminished, the posse either found that the defenders had been suddenly too well reinforced to allow chance of success, or else that the place had been temporarily evacuated.

The telling of this history, here much curtailed, had consumed some time. In the midst of it, we passed the courthouse, jail and tavern that, Mr. Wright informed me, he had selected for the county-seat and given the then too pretentious name of Lancaster, and, at the story's end, we reached, ten miles along, the eastern shore of the Susquehanna.

" Now," said Mr. Wright, " we must, for the time, separate."

The moon was now very brilliant, and it painted all that lay before us in a sort of argent noonday. From a spot of high ground, we looked down on a splendid stream. It was here perhaps a mile and a quarter wide, bordered by imposing hills that were almost mountains, rising sheer from the water and covered, save for two or three arable clearings, by mighty forests of primeval growth. Between these the river ran like fluent silver, now clear and unobstructed, again broken by a hundred jagged rocks, and yet again dotted with deeply wooded islands so close to one another that their trees must meet above the channels between them. Beautiful it was, but also mighty: even to where we passed there mounted the tumult of its thunder. The sound hung on the air as though from a great drum beaten continuously.

Mr. Wright was pointing to a most extensive clearing by the waterside: a rich plantation in which, among numerous outbuildings, rose a long, narrow, two-story house of stone exactly like those of so many country-gentlemen in Yorkshire—and, I have since heard, in Lancashire as well, which was the Wrights' place of origin.

"That," he continued, "is my house. Your uncle's lies somewhat farther along the stream, and the road thither branches off just here."

Then he looked up at some slight noise, and there, issuing from an almost invisible bridle-path, rode Uncle Simon.

We all hurried up to him and found him exhibiting few ill effects of his more roundabout, but more expeditious, journey. He said that he "knew his way about" and, indeed, he looked it. While he was asking what damage we had suffered at the hands of the highwayman, the sensation struck me that Mr. Wright could have endured his continued absence.

"On my own part, I have had only to ride quickly," the Ranger explained.

"Thee started at a good pace when thee left us," the Magistrate dryly answered.

My uncle passed by this rebuke. "I carry," said he, "certain papers of importance belonging to the government of this Commonwealth, and I fear I am being followed." He licked his thin lips. "I believe that yon highwayman was Cresap himself."

"Not he," said Mr. Wright.

"How does thee know that?" My uncle bent forward in his saddle. "Neither of us has yet seen the fellow face to face, and this man was masked."

The master of Hempfield was gathering up his reins. "Cresap's methods are notoriously brutal; whatever that masked man may now be, he was born and bred a gentleman."

But Uncle Simon put this by.

"I tell thee anyhow," he pleaded, "that I am in danger. I have been attacked. I say that there is somewhat should be guarded—my house should have a better guard." Quickly he put out a hand. "Thee has more servants than I.—I appeal to thee as to a Magistrate to lend me a guard for my state papers!"

"Guard! But thee has never before——"

Uncle Simon was almost in tears.

"My papers have never before been threatened!"

"What has thee to guard?"

THE RANGER OF THE SUSQUEHANNOCK

It was now too dark to see my uncle's face, and yet I think that, at this query, the pale spaces of his cheeks must have grown as red as the hillocks of pimples around them. I felt shame for him as he stammered:

"That is a government matter. I repeat that I have never before been threatened!"

Mr. Wright's temper—always, I fancy, a little difficult to control—again broke free.

"This," he cried, "is the veriest poltroonery! The highwayman was solitary, and thee has a houseful of servants. No, Friend Simon, I'll none of it!"

He turned his horse's head away. A moment more and a bend of the road hid him.

I looked at Uncle Simon. Fright had given way to a weak rage, cunning was replaced by a spite that turned my stomach. He peered at the spot whence the Magistrate had departed.

"Ah, ban!" he chattered, forsaking his Quaker speech and lapsing into pure Yorks. "Gawn yer way, you boomp—ye! One o' these times, t'Marylanders mon attack your mighty Hempfield. An' think ye then *I'll* send sarvents to *your* rescue? Ma faith, I'll see ye and your boorsome hoose fair burnt to t'ground first!"

CHAPTER XI

1 BOY: 7 YRS.: £2!

I RECOLLECT being in no pleasant state of mind toward my uncle as we now proceeded in the direction of "Lynton," which was the name of his estate. While we are young, we look for all the virtues in our elders and are hugely surprised and disappointed if we fail to find them there; nor is there any virtue that a boy sets above courage. Through his plea for a guard, Uncle Simon had shown himself lacking in the quality I held most dear, and I was relieved when he evinced a desire to be alone and urged the white mare well in advance of the rest of our party.

Nevertheless, I was not much the gainer by this, for Little Jacob pushed to my side, and it is possible to imagine many a better companion than he proved to be. This giant savage, if he had not tried to kill me, had surely exhibited toward me a disposition the most cruel; I had seen him torture poor creatures that were in his power, and, more recently, had opportunity to observe him in a ruthless, if partially justified, pursuit of revenge. The passion thereof was still upon him.

"Magistrate think himself heap big man," the Susquehannock grunted scornfully. "Some day Little Jacob cut his throat!"

Looking at the Indian, I had no doubt but that he meant what he said. His good eye glowered like the eyes of a catamount, and his grin was a deal more hideous than any frown.

"Mr. Wright," I ventured, "wanted no unnecessary bloodshed."

Little Jacob grinned the more. "Some night like this I catch him from behind on dark road like this. Then I cut out his heart."

"How can you talk so?" I demanded, disgust overcoming, for the moment, every fear. "I shall tell this to Mr. Scull!"

Either because my uncle was far in advance of us, or that the Susquehannock felt secure to display his effrontery when he was in his own countryside, he showed no dread of my threat. His natural state never portrays the red man a blasphemer, but this one had learned oaths from his lowest white acquaintances, and not among the roughest of our soldiery have I ever heard such vile abuse as, totally disregarding my warning, he now heaped upon the Quaker magistrate who had balked the satisfaction of his thirst for blood.

He drew a sort of vicarious delight from the doubtless evident effect that his murderous utterances had on me. When I tried to ride ahead, he suited his horse's pace to mine, and finally, with overbearing impudence, he laid his grasp on my stallion's rein.

I think that, terrible as he was, I should have struck

him then, but my faithful animal and our nearness to
our destination put a temporary end to our difficulties.
The stallion, realizing that the hand was inimical,
darted forward as if its touch had been that of a spur,
and before I could be overtaken, I was arrived close
behind my uncle, at the gates of " Lynton."

The house stood perhaps a hundred yards from the
highway. It fronted a lawn curtained therefrom by a
natural growth of melancholy pines and capped a hill
that sloped in terraces and policies to the river, whence
now a thin fog was climbing. From the rear, an an-
cient oak, spared by the builders, spread wide limbs
above a rambling two-story dwelling of gray stone,
rarely more than one room deep, but very long and
topped by the luxury of brick chimneys, the material
for which had been imported from England, as, indeed,
the whole place was purchased from a sale of the family-
lands there. It was large enough to quarter a regiment,
with wings and gables among which I felt that a boy
could easily be lost, and with a steeply-pitched shingle-
roof, whispering of mysterious attics; yet, big as it
bulked in the night, it seemed to house nobody. As we
approached, no servants came out to meet us; not even
a dog barked its welcome—I have heard that the Ranger
differed from most pioneers in disliking all canine creatures—nor were there any lights visible in the panes.

Uncle Simon had dismounted and opened, with a
great key, the front door, which I observed to be of

thick oak. It was cut across the middle, so that the lower half could be kept closed and used as a protection across which defenders could shoot at any enemy, and it was possible to reinforce the lock by an oaken bar that stood ready to fit into iron staples on either side.

So much, in the clear night, I saw as I got from my stallion. Then my uncle turned and caught sight of me.

Throughout all our journey together, his attitude toward me—though sometimes hinting a deeper condition—had been, on the surface, in keeping with our natural relationship; now, however, that I was safe within his gates there appeared a thorough, if perhaps transient, change.

" Go in by the other way," he said shortly, and called to the approaching Susquehannock: " Jacob, take him into the kitchen! "

I was too mightily astonished by this dismission to protest against it. While the Shawanese hurried the wagon and horses, not without objections from my stallion, toward a near-by stable, far behind which clustered their own huts and those of their invisible fellows, Little Jacob took my arm, in a clasp that became a biting grip, and marching me to an end of the house, opened a door scarcely less formidable than the front one. He showed me inside, followed me and closed it.

" Massáya," he said in English and with a smoldering scorn of me, "here is boy. All white men have white liver—even good Master. Had to bring."

I was in a large room. It had a low ceiling and was filled with eye-smarting smoke from a huge fireplace that held a fire ludicrously small.

From before this a woman turned.

"You talk Susquehannock," she commanded. She herself at once slipped into that tongue.

She was so tall that I thought her head—a mass of snake-locks—about to bash itself against the blackened rafters—and I wished it would!

For here was evidently Little Jacob's squaw, and enough like him to be his twin sister, and those physical qualities and moral deformities which were terrifying in the man became doubly repellent in the woman. I felt that she could tear me limb from limb with scarce an effort and with no regret: her gigantic frame had all her husband's strength. She possessed his knobby, evil face, and her grin revealed fangs the doubles of his. This was the "good wife" that my uncle had spoken of, who would "see to a boy's comfort"! He had said somewhat of her "kindly eye": that she had two good eyes, instead of one blind, was her single point of difference from her ruffian spouse—and I ought not to call them "good eyes," for they were as evil as if they burnt in the head of the Enemy of Mankind.

All this I saw while the precious pair, with frequent

glances toward me, conversed together in their native tongue. Abruptly then the talk ceased.

"You come," said Little Jacob.

Stooping to pass a low doorway, he led me, behind the fireplace, into a cell-like, unplastered room. It held no furniture. For bed, a pile of sacking lay on the stone floor.

"What's this?" I asked, and I pressed a hand to my heart, which beat hammer-blows against my ribs.

"This your room." His cold scorn flashed to an anger the more repulsive because of that one rolling eyeball's gargoyle independence. "All time boy in service, him sleep here."

The sight of the place was worse than my dread of the Indian.

"Service?" I protested, for the word gravelled me. "What do you mean by saying that I am to be in service?"

Little Jacob folded his arms and leaned against the window.

"You think Simon Scull pay all that much money for little boy just to feed? You short two pound on big canoe. Simon pay that. So he buy boy, boy sign paper, and paper say all good, boy satisfied: law-paper —make you servant seven year. Seven year!" The giant broke into raucous laughter. "No big man stand seven year slave Simon Scull: you die heap soon!"

CHAPTER XII

UNCLE SIMON'S STRONG-BOX

THE Indian was grimacing in a loathsome relish of the fright that his words had conjured. He was an adept in the black arts of torment, but for once he had forgotten that there is a point at which sheer desperation will shock the paralysis of terror into dangerous activity. To this point he had forced me. The door hung loose; I seemed to recollect another door in the kitchen, which must communicate with the body of the house. Resolved to face my uncle and learn the worst of my situation, I now made a spring into the room we had just left.

The squaw Massáya confronted me; she was lifting a great kettle of some steaming mixture from the fire. Close behind me stormed Little Jacob. I saw, to the woman's right, the exit I sought.

There was no time to lose. Like a dog-circled hare on the hillside, I scampered nimbly forward and flanked Massáya. This left naught but thin air 'twixt her and her husband, and he, having flung himself so mightily in pursuit of me, could not immediately check his chase. He collided with the squaw, and the hot soup—if soup it was she carried—fell and splashed over the pair of them. Under cover of this catastrophe and the consequent riot of their tongues—each shrieking pain and each accusing the other—I bounded into the apartment that I had been looking for.

Clearly the dining-room of " Lynton," it was fitted out with a great table of black walnut and many Jacobean chairs; but it was large enough to serve as a sort of office, too, and in a corner, at a tall desk with candles on it sate my Uncle Simon, examining a mass of papers. He half started up at the noise of my entrance, his bleared eyes narrowed.

" What's this? " he demanded. " What is thee doing here, and what is all this clamor? "

" Uncle," I cried, " Little Jacob says you have bought me, and that I must be a servant to you for seven years! "

Back of me came the Susquehannock. His iron hand closed on my squirming shoulder. It must have been soup that his wife carried: I could smell it on him now.

Uncle Simon looked at the pair of us. His mouth worked. Finally he said to Little Jacob:

" The boy had best be left in no doubt. Go! "

Jacob obeyed. I was again alone with the master of " Lynton."

" Repeat," he ordered, " what thee said a moment since."

His words to the Indian had left me little hope, but I did as bidden. " And I know you paid two pounds," I concluded, " and for that I am grateful; but, oh,

Uncle, this thing can't be true.—It is not true, is it, Uncle? "

I believe he had been all the while trying to gird himself into a rage. He flared at me:

" Does thee think I paid too much? Aye, I bought service of thee, young scoundrel! I am the more in an error or thee was lucky to escape thus a charge of mutiny—and thee signed the paper willingly."

Anger scorched my cheeks:

" But you are my uncle! Do you mean that you really bought me? You tricked me ——"

He silenced my outburst with the raising of a skinny hand.

" Gently—gently! There was no trickery. It was all writ fair and bold under the sign of the Blue Anchor Tavern. Don't pretend thee did not know."

" Then," said I, " let me see the paper."

It was one of those that he had been examining on my precipitate entrance. He answered me by lifting it from the tall desk's flap.

" But I shall hold it while thee reads," he smiled.

Of course he feared that I meant to destroy it, so he kept a tight grasp of the document, and I was compelled to bend my face close to his pimpled face as I read. My heart sank into my boots, for, though I then knew nothing of legal matters or indentured servants, this instrument which I had witlessly signed appeared to be all that he maintained for it.

So Little Jacob had spoken truth! It was as much as I could do to stifle a sob, and my uncle saw it, but what he did not surmise was that it was a sob of rage.

"I lent thee the money," he said, "because thee is thy father's son. All I demand is payment, rightful and honest. Would thee have me use thee as a pauper and give charity to a Rowntree?"

I know not if he deliberately provoked my pride. His own, such as he had, was of a curious variety, and not being of my blood, but only a step-uncle, he could understand us stiff-necked Rowntrees from observation alone. Nevertheless, it was my pride that his jeer fired, and this flamed out at him. It burnt up fear of Simon Scull and his Susquehannocks; it all but consumed my anger.

"If two pounds," said I, "can be a proper price for seven years' service, and if the bargain was honestly made, why then I will serve you seven years!"

He blinked at me, considering. He rubbed his long fingers over his long chin. I made sure he sought for a trap in my promise, and this the more hardened my pride, since I had spoken, if madly, at least in good faith. All that he said, however, was:

"I shall set thee thy tasks on the morrow. Return now to thy bedchamber."

I passed through the kitchen, under the dark silence of Little Jacob and Massáya, and entered again what I already called my cell. That name was not wholly justified, since the window was unbarred and there was no lock, either to keep me in or—what I could have wished—to shut the house-servants out. I supposed that the wild nature of the surrounding country and my ignorance of its people were deemed sufficient outer bolts and bars; and yet I was not unhappy to reach the chamber, for it provided a modicum of privacy, and I wanted to be alone. I ate some bread and cheese that Jacob brought me—he swore horribly because there was no soup for anyone—and, when he had left me, I said my prayers and, throwing myself upon the apology for a bed, began confusedly to consider my plight.

What whirled through my fevered mind was neither ordered thinking nor did it lead anywhither. I accused myself of blindness for not having read that paper before giving it my signature; then asked how I could have escaped Grimshaw without signing it, and finally excused my action because I had been dealing with my only relative in the New World, and him an officer of the Province.

I thought of appealing to the Lord Proprietor to ask if all were regular, and remembered the wilderness that separated us—said I would seek Magistrate Wright, yet knew in my heart the document was legal. And all the while, that pride of mine imperiously commanded me to work-out this usury and serve my term. I was brave, I was strong, I was young; I could survive and, worshipping my father's memory, I was resolved to do naught that could bring discredit on his name. A prisoner he was, but a prisoner for his faithful, our rightful King: I would have no charge of moral turpitude laid against his son.

The night was now well advanced, midnight must have long gone upon the clock—and, late as was the season, thunder hung in the air—a thing that has ever sorely oppressed me, man and boy; so, though I at last gave over my maddening speculations, the time was long before I could find sleep.

There were at first noises in the kitchen, where Massáya clattered pots and pans, and she and Little Jacob scolded each other in their barbarous tongue; chants discordant and drunken floated, now and again, from the huts where the Shawanese were quartered, and once, after all this had subsided into a silence like that of death—a silence worse than the noises—I was jumped out of my bed by the scream of a screech-owl, or of some wild animal in the neighboring forest.

I tossed and dozed and woke again. The thunder rumbled afar, but drawing ever nearer. The room was black as pitch; I would fancy a movement at the door, but, when I crept out of bed and stole to it, the latch was down, and I did at last sink into a stupor of exhaustion.

What followed may have had its origin in the last sounds of which I was conscious before falling asleep: the hastily built frontier house creaked in the rising wind; it cried out like the timbers of the *John and Anne* in a heavy swell, and I began to dream I was again aboard of her. I lived over my perilous voyage, but with nightmare additions. The Stranger was not there to protect me, but my big, kindly father was a prisoner aboard, and I with him. I thought that Grimshaw had put gyves on us and bound us to the mizzen, and finally I heard padding feet on the deck. All I could move was my eyes, but, turning them, I seemed to see Captain Warcut, all dripping water and, though drowned, advancing toward me with a drawn knife. I sat bolt upright in bed, only to realize that, an indentured servant, I was little better off here in "Lynton" than I had been on that immigrant-ship at sea.

I was now broad awake, yet convinced that there had been some foundation in reality for my dream. The thunder rattled. Was there anybody else in my room? A flash of lightning assured me that the cell was empty.

I went to the window. The earth was ink; the sky arace with galloping clouds. In the pauses between thunder-peals, the whole house complained; no single sound was unaccountable, but I had a vivid sense of stealthy movement somewhere close at hand.

I waited, trembling. Finally I was rewarded: soft footsteps sounded overhead.

On such occasions, one does not reason, and this is well, for reason is an opiate to action. One acts upon the result of all previous training and habit of body and mind, which is the best reason for thinking and doing bravely in periods of quiet, since only thus one behaves like a man in the instant of crisis. I was a boy and not such a fool as not to know fear, but my upbringing had given me hard and nimble muscles and a brain that could face realized danger. I told myself that no honest man would move with such caution as I heard on the floor above.

I took it for certain that there was a thief in the house. If, as I suspected and, indeed, hoped, it was Little Jacob, then I should ease my lot by exposing him to dismissal at Uncle Simon's hands; if it was somebody else, I should still raise myself in my relative's favor by seizing the intruder. In any case, since I was in service, I owed a duty to my master and would do it —and in any case also, you may be sure, not the least compelling of my motives was that species of boyish curiosity which is stronger than any dread.

Softly I opened the door and passed into the kitchen.

Twice the thunder startled me into stillness, as if directed for my correction alone; once the lightning must have revealed me, had there been anybody at hand to see; but I made a rapid progress, though a groping one, and so found the door into the dining-room. I crossed that apartment and came into the hall.

It was me the lightning now assisted. In its flash, I saw a steep stairway, mounting to the upper floor and thence, presumably, to the loft. And through the succeeding blackness I heard that cunning footfall creeping toward the roof.

Again, and in a very spasm of attention, I waited. Far above, a door was opened and guardedly closed: the door, it must be, of an attic.

Then I followed. The stairs creaked under me, and I had to make many a pause, but it seemed that none heard me, and, in a sweat of excitement, I achieved the ascent. It terminated on a short landing before a closed portal, through a crack below which came a gleam of yellow light.

The thunder banged above the roof, over which the old oak-tree's limbs groaned in the pauses, rheumatically. I bent to a faint keyhole; the key had been removed without relocking, but the intruder was somewhere outside the narrow range of vision then afforded: I saw only a dim section of the sort of attic to be expected in a pioneer's house, filled with the expected lumber. As I rose, the long-gathering storm broke in a tremendous crash; under cover of that cachinnation, I pushed the door ajar and obtained a full view of the attic and its sinister intruder.

There he was, crouched beside a big strong-box. The man whom I had followed was Uncle Simon himself!

CHAPTER XIII

" IN WHOSE NAME? "

EVEN so. In an obscure corner, not fifteen feet from where my amazement straightway rooted me, a flickering candle stood on the loose planks of the floor, dangerously close to the low eaves. It showed my uncle's meagre form, swathed only in a nightgown, a high-peaked nightcap on his head and tied beneath his chin, kneeling by an open, iron-bound chest stuffed with documents. From among these, he had dug up and unlocked a metal case of more portable size containing other papers, to which he was adding one that I recognized as the ill-starred instrument signed by me at the Blue Anchor.

I caught my breath sharply. I was for backing out of the attic and retreating to bed as circumspectly as I had advanced; but before I could budge to that impulsion, I had observed Uncle Simon's next movement and was fastened to the spot.

From under his nightshirt, he drew the bulging money-belt that I had noted when he was thrown by his horse, and out of it now fell something that caught my eye and was clutched by him as if it were his own tumbling soul. He laid it in the metal box and then

102

slowly proceeded to place beside it its companions from the belt.

I can smell the stuffy air, can hear the rain on the shingles, I can see the picture of that attic as if it all were dated yesterday: the steeply sloping roof, the vast shadowy room with its dusty stowage; its unfinished flooring unnailed and loose; the tossing candle flame that gave a circle of light; the chest within this, and by the chest gaunt Uncle Simon kneeling in his shift, now plucking at the belt, now peering at what he withdrew and again depositing the withdrawals, piece by piece, in the metal box.

He bent near the flame to squint at them out of his red-rimmed eyes, and so presented toward me his profile. Into his pimpled face had crept a hideous tenderness, such as a witch-wife might exhibit when looking at the sleep of her evil brats whom she plans to rear in her own practices. Laid in their new hiding-place, the objects of my strange uncle's solicitude formed a glittering mass of brilliants that even the startled boy at the door at once realized as almost priceless jewels.

Though the events of my ocean-voyage had somewhat cowed me, and the novelty of the new country obscured my natural keenness, these were but a passing ailment, which time and the happenings of the present night were conjoining rapidly to cure. I was never any man's fool for long, and now began to emerge from the spell of my uncle. I was not yet, as you will see, wholly recovered, but I was near enough that state to ask myself some very pertinent questions.

Here, plainly, I had surprised a secret, and how was the secret to be accounted for? Pennsylvania was a rude colony, a far vidette of civilization, where jewels of any high value were all but unknown: how, in such a wilderness, did these come to Simon Scull's possession?

Had he purchased them in Philadelphia? There could not be their like in all the New World.

Had he got them by the *John and Anne?* His regard of them was that of a familiar.

Their price, I reckoned, would exceed the estate of "Lynton" a hundredfold: how could they, then, have been honestly come by?

I had been clutching the door in the unconscious continuance of my purpose to close it after me as a guard to my retreat, but now that protection became my betrayal. A quick gust of storm-wind broke a window on the stairway, rushed past me, whipped the door from my hand and all but extinguished my uncle's clandestine candle.

Uncle Simon looked over his shoulder to determine the origin of the draft. I scuttled back to the landing, but there came through that broken window a flash, which painted me clear in the very act of flight.

He saw me. All in the twinkling of an eye, his countenance passed to a tragic amazement—to a tragic resolution. He leaped.

I have presented him as a coward, and so, in what one may call the beginnings of things, he was. He would, as I later discovered, plan with daring equalled only by his ingenuity; then craft would swell to timidity at the launching; but once his scheme was afloat and he irretrievably aboard, he was capable of a courage almost heroic. This was now the case. I had a manifest advantage in strength, yet, upon the instant of discovery, he cast himself at me without flicker of hesitation and with an agility astounding in a man of his age.

His fingers fastened on my throat. He was between me and the candle, so that I could not see his face, but his rank breath beat against my nostrils in gusts of rage. The attack utterly bewildered me; it was mere preservative instinct that flung my hands to his and, as I pulled for release, twisted a leg around his straining shanks.

He tried to cry out. I thought of Little Jacob and spared one palm to clap it over his mouth. Then, with a crash, we fell together to the landing and rolled down the stairs.

Only the level of the second story stopped our descent, and that none too securely. There we writhed and fought a moment, like cats in the dark; but our descent (which had freed his mouth, yet left him, for the nonce, no breath for shouting) loosed also his pressure of my wind-pipe.

"Uncle," I panted and my thick tongue clove to the roof of my mouth, "don't you know me?"

Ere he could answer, there came a rush of moccasined feet on the stairs. An eye that could see in the night picked me out; arms of metal seized me: the Susquehannock lifted me and held me as if I were not more than a struggling child.

"Hum!" he grunted. "Mebbe now Master say Little Jacob right!"

Uncle Simon said nothing. I heard him stumble to his feet; I felt the Indian's grip tighten; I smelled the fumes of stale liquor and knew that he was in his most diabolical mood.

"Little Jacob kill?" he asked. Never was voice more cruel or cold. "This time kill sure!"

The reply came not from my uncle; it came from outside the house. The storm had been as brief as violent; already it had subsided, but at the great oak door of entrance to the hall there roared another sort of thunder: the thunder of a tremendous triple-knock.

"Whad gooes theer?" My uncle had found voice at last, and found it in his native Yorkshire speech.

The Indian dropped me. "I go see."

"Whist!" cautioned the Ranger.

Enemies a moment since, we began to tiptoe together down the remaining flight of stairs.

" Soft! " my uncle continued. " Happen whoever 'tis'll think there be no one here."

But the knock was repeated. The hall echoed to it.

" Open! " cried a mighty voice.

" There is a lanthorn on the table," whispered Uncle Simon to his steward. " Light it."

The thing was done. My uncle took the lanthorn then, having turned the key in its lock, his free hand on the oaken bar that still held the door.

" Who's there? " he quavered, " that disturbs the sleep of a peaceable planter on this stormy night? "

Through the heavy door pierced imperatively that repeated command:

" Open! "

We on the inside were a party for a tableau. There stood Little Jacob, but grinning now in uncertainty; there stood I, doubtless considerably disarranged from my recent tussle, and there, too, Uncle Simon, his peaked nightcap askew, but still upon his head, and the lanthorn that he held trembling so that the shadows danced a hornpipe across the walls.

An instant his mouth worked, and then emitted a hollow question:

" In whose name? "

From behind the big portal the loud voice sounded once again, and none the more assuring for its mocking laughter:

" In any name you like! How suits you this?—

'Open in the name of your brother and my friend, Francis James Rowntree, Earl of Ravenscar!'"

At that, the lanthorn in Uncle Simon's hand shook more violently than ever, and I saw his face turn the color of lead. Hoarsely, he issued an order to the Susquehannock:

"Get the boy into the kitchen and see that he stays there!"

As Little Jacob dragged me away, I heard the front door swing wide.

CHAPTER XIV

RED SEALING-WAX

FIRST there in the hall, then during my compulsory passage through the dining-room and finally in the kitchen, my ears served me well that night. There was little to be gained by a struggle with the Indian, so that I went quietly enough, though as laggardly as I dared, and, as we passed between the table and that desk at which my uncle had, earlier, let me read my sentence of servitude, I heard, in answer to the natural question, our nocturnal visitor's voice furnish a reason for his appearance at " Lynton ": he was, he said, an unhorsed traveller, who sought shelter from the storm.

The words of Uncle Simon's response were not distinct to me, and must have evidenced some hesitation, perhaps pointing out that the rain was over, for the self-invited guest boomed at him:

" Do I look like one that will stand here the rest of the night at parley? Had not the wet spoiled my priming, I should enforce entrance with my pistols—with my sword, but for scorn to soil good steel in the skewering of carrion. Stand aside and let me in ! "

At this, in the dining-room with Little Jacob's hands upon me, I could feel that the Susquehannock debated whether to complete obedience of his master's orders or return to his rescue. But my uncle's next words were audible and determined the continuation of our retreat: the unarmed Ranger—whom I could fancy cringing in flapping nightclothes at the door—protested that he had meant no lack of hospitality; studiously avoiding, as it seemed to me, reference to that recent mention of my father, he invited entrance, and then cried out to my warden to waken Massáya and fetch some refreshment to the dining-room.

So I was passed on to the kitchen, where I found me a chair opposite the hearth. Candles were lit, the squaw summoned and preparations made to feed the guest.

Amid these, and the quarrels that readily engendered between husband and wife, I was all but forgotten, and made the most of that neglect. I heard my uncle and the newcomer in the dining-room; scraps of talk, at first formal and meaningless, floated occasionally from them to me. At last, by quietly edging my chair in the desired direction, I was in place to obtain a view beyond the door whenever Little Jacob, in serving, opened it, and so, within some twenty minutes, I made a not unexpected discovery.

The two men sat there at the now well-lighted table. Uncle Simon, who had been fetched a dust-colored dressing-gown, gave his stooped back to my gaze; but the face of the man opposite was fully illuminated by the candles and as clear as a vivid portrait set in a black frame. Dark, imperious, domineering, eagle-eyed, his voice had already given me a clue: if this was not our masked highwayman of the Wilderness Road, yet certainly it was that Stranger who had saved me on the ship, the swarthy and exulting demigod whom I had last had clear sight of when he repelled the port-officers and plunged to safety in the Delaware from the rail of the *John and Anne.*

Little Jacob, coming out, closed the door on this confirmation. He cast a suspicious glance at me, but was diverted by some criticism from his squaw, and when next he returned to the dining-room, I heard Uncle Simon saying something to the Stranger about the port of Philadelphia, which led me to believe that recognition was not mine alone. Nevertheless, everything that I observed pointed to a peace around the supper-table, and presently I could make out my uncle excusing himself and ambling to his desk. On the next opening of the door, I smelled sealing-wax.

It was but little later that the master of the house came into the kitchen. He closed the door behind him and beckoned me to a corner.

" Nephew," says he, and he patted my head with a long hand, " thee gave me a grand start a while back. Had not faithful Jacob appeared, I might have done thee bodily harm in the belief that some robber was upon me."

But for Little Jacob's coming, it was I who might have hurt my uncle; yet to this it would be idle to refer. Something else was uppermost.

"Why, sir," said I, "I called out to you it was I."

He shook his still nightcapped head. "Then that was after I had attacked thee, and I was too bent upon self-protection to heed. Nicholas," he went on, with a sharp gaze at me, "what prompted thee to play the spy?"

I declared that I was no spy, and told him how I had thought there was a thief abroad in the house.

"And what"—his fingers twitched, and he leaned the nearer—"what," says he, licking at his lips, "did thee see?"

I will not defend the lie I told him. I felt safe so long as my former friend was in the dining-room, and yet I had a clear sense that my future would be less secure than that of another indentured servant were I to admit a knowledge of the Ranger's secret. The right course had been to tell the truth and then, if need be, summon the Stranger's help. All that I may plead is thoughtlessness—although the poorest of excuses,—and so says I:

"Nothing but what you know."

"Thee had just reached the landing?" my uncle persisted.

Heartily ashamed, yet feeling myself now committed, I could only nod.

He seemed satisfied. He remonstrated against what he was pleased to call my foolish fears and my tendency toward night-wandering, yet he spoke kindly enough, and it was only when he commanded me to indulge in such practices no more that his tone became severe.

"This is a rough country," he straightway explained, "and men act violently in what they think to be protection of their own. Next time thee's frightened of marauders, lie still and call for Little Jacob, or thee might thyself be again mistaken for the subject of thy own fears and that time meet a bullet in the dark."

I know now that my safety rested in his persistent assumption of my being a stupid boy, but I was then indignant that he should think cowardly an action that still seemed to me, if mistaken, yet brave. Nevertheless, I shall not say that I wholly believed his story of not recognizing me; I had to give him what the lawyers call "the benefit of the doubt," but because it was a doubt, I thought best to hold my tongue and let the adventure pass with as little talk as might be.

"Yes, sir," says I.

"Not 'sir,'" he corrected. "I am now, like the Lord Proprietor, a member of the Society of Friends, and we hold by no worldly titles. Not 'sir,' nephew, but 'uncle.'"

So said I: "Yes, uncle"—and I did not relish the saying of it.

"And now," he went on, "I have thy first task for

thee—somewhat sooner than I expected. Thee has proved an excellent horseman: thee mount thy stallion immediately and deliver this letter."

From the pocket of his dressing-gown he drew a missive, the cause, no doubt, of his having left the table and gone to his desk. The address was as yet hidden, but the candlelight fell on the paper, and it was sealed with red wax that looked like a great splash of blood.

" I may spare none of the Shawanese," he continued; " they have a heavy day's farm-work before them, and it is written ' Thou shalt not muzzle the ox when he treadeth out the corn '; and as for Little Jacob, he must remain to attend our guest."

He held out the letter. There was, however, one question that postponed my acceptance.

" Why," I asked, " did this guest come in my father's name? "

Uncle Simon half drew back the missive. Then he smiled and shook his head as one reproves a too inquisitive child:

" It is in connection therewith that I am having thee go upon this errand. The secret is thy father's and my guest's, and I am scarce at liberty to reveal it."

" But I know your guest," says I.

" What's this? " says Uncle Simon, very quickly.

Since my uncle, whatever his purpose toward me, was

now acting for the Stranger, I saw no harm in telling the facts. They fell from me, at all events, spontaneously:

" He is the gentleman that saved me on the *John and Anne.*"

" Ha! " snapped Uncle Simon. " I thought as much." His mouth worked a moment. " Why then," he resumed, " thee will be the readier to help him. We shall not inquire into those of his difficulties that are no concern of ours, but we owe him the more since he is not only thy father's friend, but thine as well.—Come now," says he, propelling me toward the door to the yard. " To horse!—Jacob, where is this key? My nephew rides to Lancaster."

I could not press for revelation of a secret the preservation of which, even from me, seemed to assist my father's welfare, but there was still some hesitancy in me.

" Lancaster? " I repeated. " You forget that I am a stranger to these roads."

But Uncle Simon continued to speed me. " There is but one way, so far as thee need know for present purposes. It is that thee come by this evening and impossible to miss." He glanced out of a window. " Besides, the moon is now out again. Ride, and ride fast. Stop only at the first house in the next settlement after Hempfield: that will be Lancaster. Knock and ask for Charles Jones. Then deliver this letter into his hands only. Our guest demands the errand's execution before dawn."

I had no fear of dangers by the way and was glad to be of service to the man that had saved me from the bloody-handed Warcut. How this could also assist the cause of my father, a prisoner across the sea, was more than it was possible for me to imagine, but I had not for nothing lived half my boyhood in a land still full of Jacobite plottings; I had heard how politics worked deviously, and I was my father's son.

"Very good, uncle," said I; "there shan't be rein drawn until I shall have reached Lancaster."

CHAPTER XV

A PRICE ON HIS HEAD

AS I walked my stallion past " Lynton's " gate, held open by morose Little Jacob—the good horse had refused his saddle from other hands than mine,—one look overshoulder showed me a candle passing from window to window in the upper floor of the house: that would be Uncle Simon lighting his guest to a bedchamber. The glow stopped in the north corner of the west wing, well removed, so far as my knowledge went, from the apartments used by the customary inhabitants: there the Stranger was to rest. Then the gate closed, and I turned into the once more moonlit road.

Uncle Simon had been correct: there was no chance of going wrong, and this because, except at that fork whence a way led to " Hempfield," only one road, the well remembered one, existed; the woods closed close 'round it on either hand. I had no difficulty about my course.

Of the ten miles of my ride down to Lancaster I have few recollections—perhaps for something the same reason as I have few of my state of mind after my presentation to the Lord Proprietor in Philadelphia;

perhaps because I retain such lively pictures of my journey back—but I do remember that never a dread rode with me, and that my heart grew unaccountably lighter with each blow of the bay stallion's hoofs. So beautiful was now the night, so sweet-smelling the earth after rain and so deep the sense of freedom in the air, that, had I not guessed the formal legality of my indenturing, had I known some refuge to seek, and had I not thought my father's cause and the Stranger's case might require my further service, temptation had assailed my pride and its promise to Uncle Simon: I should have been prompted to run away as soon as that red-sealed letter was delivered.

Howbeit, I came to Lancaster. The woods ended abruptly in a cleared field that reached to the tavern I had noted in the afternoon: a log-house huddling against a somewhat larger one-storied building in its rear. There was a light inside; I rode into a sort of courtyard and, dismounting, hurriedly hitched the bay to a convenient post.

The noise of my arrival woke a half-dozen dogs, who startled me with their clamor, but who, as it was shortly clear, were all chained and kennelled. None the less, their clatter resulted in the opening of a door. Scarce was I out of saddle ere a shadowy head appeared, and a sharp voice demanded:

"Who's this an' what d'you want?"

"Does Charles Jones live here?" I asked, advancing.

A PRICE ON HIS HEAD

I suppose because that whole countryside lay in such mortal terror of Cresap, the fellow was slow with an answer. He gave me question for question:

"The Constable of Hempfield? What d'you want of him?"

From being the name of Mr. Wright's estate, the term "Hempfield" had come to be applied to all that district. This I did not then know, but I knew the title of "constable," and, you may be sure, did not like the sound of it. I believe I should have drawn back, but now my inquisitor had laid a firm hold of me.

"Why," says I, "I have a letter for him from Ranger Simon Scull."

The man drew me inside the building and closed the door. He took me, securely held, through a brief passage connecting the tavern with the building behind it, and ushered me into a room with high barred windows, where, at a table illuminated by guttering candles erect in their own grease, two men, whose guns leaned against opposite walls, sat at cards. The cards were dirty and dog's-eared, the players were anything but prepossessing; a vacant chair told me that I had interrupted my conductor's part in the game, and, seeing those bars and having heard the word "constable," I rightly assumed that I was come to the guard-room of the county jail.

"A letter from the Ranger," explained my host. He addressed one of the seated players: a stout man, who was whistling "Lillibullero" under his breath and whose fat nose had a wart on it. "What can he want o' me at this here time o' night?"

The stomachy man, whose name was Edward Cartlidge, an Indian-trader, wheezed: "Mote look an' see, Charley."

His neighbor, whom they were soon calling Samuel Chance, and whom I set down as a half-breed, added:

"Why he send some stranger?" His mouth had been once hacked by a knife, and the scar dragged down a corner.

I hastened to explain my relationship to Simon Scull and my recent arrival in the Colony.

"Well," says my host, "I'm Constable Jones, so these news are for me. Out with this here letter!"

There was nothing to do but hand it over. Jones lit a pipe and, bending to one of the candles, broke that red seal. He was a little fellow, but wiry; his hair was yellow, yet his face had been burnt black by long exposure to the sun, and he had eyes that looked as if they could gimlet through iron.

"It's Simon's own hand o' write," he said.

Cartlidge yawned and shuffled the cards. "If Scull," says he lazily, "wasn't so clever and conscientious at his duties, a better man would hold his office. Nobody loves him. But night and day he works. What's this he has to say now, Charley?"

Jones's glance leapt from the paper and bored through me. He laid aside his pipe.

" First o' all, he says the boy's not to know—might be frightened."

The half-breed took my measure. " Him no coward," he grunted.

" I am not indeed! " I cried.

" Oh," Cartlidge growled, " don't mind Simon. This is but another of his cries of ' Wolf ' when there is no wolf. Let's hear it and get on with the game."

" Orders is orders," said the wiry Constable, and flung the letter on the table.

But Uncle Simon's command that I be kept in ignorance of his message had been written without counting upon the Indian-trader. Picking up the letter, he grumbled: " You have a dozen times told him, Charley, that you would not come to him again o' night to catch anyone less than Thomas Cresap himself. Why, Charley ——" And then the protest died on his lips and his eyes bulged at the paper. He sprang up, oversetting his chair. " Sam," he shouted to the half-breed Chance, " by the Eternal, here's clever Simon with Cresap locked up in the house of ' Lynton ' and waiting for Jones and a posse! "

" The boy—the boy! " Jones warned him.

" Oh, blast the boy! " All trace of phlegm had fled this heavy trader now. " Here, Charley, think of the reward. Raise a pair of your nearest neighbors; only a pair: the more to share, the less to pay! "

It was upon me to speak out my certainty that Uncle

Simon must be mistaken, yet I knew in my heart that here was no error, but a lie, and, had not shame for my relative bound my tongue, sheer wonder at such life-and-death treachery had dumbfounded me. I sought to speak out, but only stuttered nothings, which none heeded; and just then there burst another chorus of dogs from the court and a clatter of horses on the road, immediately followed by a running in the passage. Two men, their eyes starting out of the sockets, pushed into the room.

"Jones," the first newcomer shouted, "he's at it ag'in, the varmint!"

He was a fine-looking fellow, goodish large, with long whisps of flame-red hair sticking from under his coonskin cap, and the other man, evidently his servant, for all his frontier garments, just such a ruddy Yorkshireman as might have been a gamekeeper at Castle Wyke.

"Cresap?" asked the Constable. He ran his fingers through his yellow hair. "You mean Cresap?"

"Sure an' whom else?" The speaker's Irish face was as hot with indignation as with the exertions of his ride. "Him er his under-divils. Late this afternoon 'twas, an' we safe indoors, you may wager, at our tea. Eight of me horses they hamstringed and got away before we heard a whimper."

Cartlidge had paused, puffing, at my elbow, and I asked him who this was.

"Jimmie Patterson," the windy trader told me, "and

his servant, Knowles Daunt. Patterson has a Susquehanna plantation—the east-bank—he keeps pack-horses bought from the reds down along the Potomac."

But Constable Jones was saying: "Well, he'll hamstring no more horses after the next sun-up." His sharp eyes shone and his dark face hardened as he jerked the letter toward Patterson.

Then, thinking I saw a way to save both my benefactor's liberty and my uncle's reputation, I found tongue.

"My men," I protested, and there must have been much wonder in my sallow face and mayhap a touch of fright as well, "there's some grievous mistake here. One of you said my uncle cried 'Wolf' too readily. Well, here he is in error again, and had he confided in me, you need not have been disturbed by his letter. I know this stranger who is at 'Lynton.'"

"And what's his name?" asked the quick voice of Jones.

"That I do *not* know, but I tell you that I know the man and he cannot be Cresap because he is but now arrived in America; he voyaged on the very ship that carried me."

The five men looked at one another.

"Puff!" cried the little Constable. "You do not know his name. I do, then: 'tis Cresap. They say he's left us once ere this for Europe, but he's left his men behind him, and they're able lieutenants enough.

Where did you part from your fellow-voyager, son? I'll lay you a golden guinea he never showed himself in Philadelphia-town!"

It was then, though I know not the reason, that the under-truth of my uncle's villainy sprang as clear as clear into my comprehension. The Constable had warned him that he would make no more night-excursions to " Lynton " for any lesser catch than Cresap: very good; Simon Scull sent word that the Stranger was Cresap, merely to have him laid by the heels; once my friend was safe here in the Lancaster jail, the Ranger would admit his error and promptly have the captive held under dead Warcut's charge of mutiny on the high seas.

There was no telling that to these men. All save the servant Daunt, they ran to and fro, hooking their coats together, taking up their firearms and seeing to the priming.

" We're five now," Cartlidge was puffing, " and that's a plenty! "

He won Jones to his mercenary point of view. Already their brief preparations for the expedition must be almost complete. I was in despair. I could not see that they were only bent on rightly enforcing the law; to me the very air was heavy with treason: they were the enemies of my friend and would soon place him where a false charge would start him on the road to shameful death.

CHAPTER XVI

A RACE IN THE NIGHT

MY roving gaze fell upon Knowles Daunt. I have said that he resembled a North-Country gamekeeper. His face was a healthy red; he had a kindly eye; he reminded me of home.

He was just there at the door, waiting orders, like a good servant, where he had been left, and all the others were now talking and hustling excitedly about other parts of the room. As our glances met, I more than ever liked the look of him. He beckoned me.

"Lad," says he, "this is no place fur t'likes o' you." He spoke the familiar North-Country tongue, and spoke it not like my uncle, when that one relapsed from his Quaker phraseology, but with a kindly warmth to it. "You'd be better far abed, y'ung gentleman."

He opened the door, and I slid out. Sick at heart and with no notion of what next to do, I made my way to the courtyard.

The moon had set, and the darkness was absolute, but the dogs must have reconciled themselves to me, for the sole sound that came from them was a clanking of chains. I stumbled forward and struck against something that, in the haste of my arrival, I had not

125

observed. It was some sort of platform, and there were steps leading up to it. I felt those steps with my groping hand. Perhaps the scores of trembling feet that had pressed them left a message plainer than print upon the insensate wood. Something, in any case, spoke from them to me, for at the touch I knew what this was: it was the jail's gallows-tree.

I must have cried out in leaping away. Certainly I cried out when my backward-flung hand was met by a damp something that nosed toward it. A low whinny cut short another shriek: my honest stallion's muzzle passed up my arm and breathed caressingly against my fevered cheek.

He whinnied again, but very soft. It seemed that he felt a need for caution. I vow it seemed more: it seemed that he was whispering a plan. The strategic possibility of my position came to me, as it were, out of his nostrils. I upbraided myself for my previous stupidity; but even yet a few minutes' handicap could be gained: I would race back to "Lynton" and warn the Stranger.

I unhitched the horse. Within, they had been too occupied to hear my cries, but now Jones missed me. Above their hubbub of preparation, I heard his sharp demand:

"Where's that lanky boy? He's overfond of Cresap; I misdoubt he's set off ahead of us!"

Daunt made some soothing answer; it was ineffective.

126

A RACE IN THE NIGHT

I durst wait to hear no more; the need for caution having passed, I vaulted into my saddle and was in the act of giving the stallion my heels when Patterson's brogue arrested me:

" The gate's locked an' here's the blessed key. I was afeared thim blackguards might be followin', so I shut the yard-dure when I come in, an' thin your news startled the mimory av't out o' me."

" Then if he's gone, it's afoot."—That was Jones's voice again.—" He can climb that wall, but no horse would jump it."

Darkness—a small yard—a high wall! What was I to do? I had no conception of my mount's abilities as a jumper, yet ten long miles stretched betwixt me and " Lynton ": the thing had to be attempted.

I could not see the gate, but I knew where the road lay. Around the other horses hitched there, I backed the stallion clear of the scaffold and against the opposite wall.

The posse heard me. They ran to the door; its opening gave out a faint but helpful radiance. As they poured shouting toward me,

" Stand clear! " I yelled.

And then I gathered rein and let the horse have my heels at last.

" Success! " I called into one of his back-thrust ears.

It was a mere prayer to Heaven, but so completely did that animal comprehend my need and so instantly seek to supply it that from this moment it became my name for him.

The posse read my purpose. Fear of the horse stopped them in their tracks; their very dread of death for me was so great as to be unutterable: warning was struck dumb.

Like a ball from a musket, Success sped across the courtyard. From toe to thigh, I, bending low, glued myself to him. The wall seemed to have rushed at us. I pulled in his head:

" Jump! "

Would he refuse the gate?

He rose in air.

Could he clear the barrier?

We flew. The stallion's hoofs struck the road. It had been a frightful leap, but for a moment only did he stand atremble; then, at his best speed, we were galloping through the dark. As we went, I heard the courtyard gate swung open and knew that now my progress would be indeed a race.

I owned to sharp pictures of that breakneck return: " pictures " were a word ill-chosen, for, so deep was the night, not a thing was visible; but no second of time has ever been forgotten. If only from twice traversing it, Success knew the road: he never hesitated. He knew, too, our necessity: not one horse in a hundred, after such journeys as he had had, could have taken and held the pace that now my stallion assumed and maintained.

A RACE IN THE NIGHT

His gallop was a shooting thunder. Sparks flashed from the road; terrified echoes rolled among the hills. The wind of our flight whipped my cheeks; it buffeted the breath out of my lungs. Miles melted, and still as if it were a hated enemy, Success beat distance under his iron heels.

I shouted applause: he heard and snorted. I called encouragement: never was any required, and at last it was dissuasion that became imperative. No living thing could keep this up for long; he would kill himself. I fought him with the bit to little purpose; I protest I had to plead with him to compel him to a moment's rest.

Heaving, impatient, he cocked his ears, and I cocked mine. At first, so loud was both our breathing, I could have heard no sound of pursuit had pursuit been hard upon us; but finally I might listen fairly, and I listened in vain: the dark, last hours of the night piled into an empty dome above us, the land all silent round about— we had outraced the posse.

We proceeded then, for a little time, at a trot that Success tried always to develop into a gallop. Not until I was sure that it would be safe for him did he get his head, and we slacked again when we came to the fork in the road.

You might not say that the night was brighter, but it was a little less even as we approached our journey's end. Soon I could make out the wall of "Lynton" ahead of us. In order that the sound of Success's feet might give no alarm, I turned him into the wood and slipped from the saddle. I was badly cramped, but I climbed the gate and ran quietly along the drive. Half-way up, I remembered that, in my haste, I had omitted to tie Success: too late now; I had to go on. When I neared the house, I turned through some shrubbery and on to a lawn extending around the building.

Well was it that I had given that parting over-shoulder glance as I rode away; but for it I had not now known where the Stranger was lodged. I crept to the west wing. The night was indeed thinning: I could see his window. I felt for and found a couple of pebbles and cast one timidly at the darkened panes.

I was both overcautious and too excited: the stone fell short. I tried again, and that shot went too high. I had well outdistanced my pursuers, but I could not afford to waste moments in this fashion. Desperately I stooped and groped about for further means of communication.

The Stranger, however, must have slept as lightly as a cat. He had heard the patter of my second cast against the wall, and I had not risen before the window gently raised above me.

" Yes? "

I could not now mistake his voice:

" Come down at once and quietly! " I whispered,

dashing the sweat from my brow. " At once and quietly. They are *en route* to arrest you! They must be nearly here!"

CHAPTER XVII

PISTOLS AT THE RIVER

" A ND how do I know that? " asked the Stranger. It had not occurred to me that he might doubt my intentions. Time was slipping by; already there was a soft stir of birds among the trees. I could have cried out in chagrin. Instead whereof,

" It's true! " I whispered.

" And how came *you* to know it? "

" Because it was I ———— "

And there I stopped. If, as it seemed, he suspected that this was a ruse to rid his unwilling host of him, would he be liker to believe me when I told him of being sent by my own uncle to encompass his arrest?

My very hesitation seemed to determine him.

" I have important business in this house," he carelessly declared, " and I was just about to transact it when you disturbed me."

The pale, outstretched finger of dawn reached over the eastern horizon. In the barnyard of " Lynton " a cock crew; from somewhere in the direction of " Hempfield," another answered. As the autumnal night had been long, so the dawn came sudden. At any instant, the posse might arrive; in a few minutes, Little Jacob——

or any or all of the servants—must waken. My anxiety
became a paroxysm.

"I will tell you why you can trust me," said I: "I
am that boy you rescued aboard the *John and Anne.*"

"Why, yes," said the Stranger easily. "I knew it
when we met on yonder highroad."

It left him unmoved! "Then do I not owe you a
debt?"

"You keep strange company ashore, my lad."

Faint and far off, a new sound stole through the
quiet. I dropped flat and listened, my head against the
sward. I rose and put a hand to an ear. Then I
pointed to the road.

"Listen," said I, "and if you will not believe me,
will you believe your own senses?"

He leaned far out. He heard.

"I believe that you are speaking true," he admitted,
"and I have delayed my business too long." His cloak
was around him, his hat in his hand. He put a leisurely
leg over the sill. "But what of you?" He paused
again. "If they guess you have warned me, 'twill go
hard with you."

The sounds of the pursuit drew nearer. I fairly
danced with impatience:

"Hurry—hurry! If you are under arrest, you cannot help me."

He laughed. "We can always fight before arrest."

"Against such odds?" I wrung my hands. "Oh, hurry!"

He lowered himself from the window and dropped lightly beside me. "You could accompany me and be off before their arrival."

Never have I been so tempted, but I remembered my promise, and sheer pride saved me. Let the Constable tell my uncle what he would of my part in this escape —if escape it was to be!—I should keep my word and remain at "Lynton."

We had rounded the house and paused beneath that old oak-tree which topped it.

"I will not budge," said I. And I could now plainly hear the posse's hoof-beats on the road.

"Why so?" he asked, giving me a searching look out of his dark eyes.

"It is a matter of honor."

He smiled at my boyish earnestness, but I was sure he approved its motive. He shrugged his cloaked shoulders.

"Why, if that is so, then there is no more to say than farewell. And here's my hand, my apologies for mistrusting a gentleman and my thanks for your timely warning."

It had been none too timely, or not his slow reception of it. I heard the regular gallop of the posse as it sped toward us from the forks.

"Which way will you go?" I asked.

" The bravest general," he answered, " is the one that, in advancing, makes provision for a possible retreat. I have my retreat ready." He nodded toward the river, which the descending grounds of " Lynton " separated from the road.

It was full morning now: I looked out over the Susquehanna as it stretched, gray, beneath us. At this point, the water—it was, of course, not far above where the ferry runs to-day—is, as you know, nigh a mile and a half wide, unobstructed by the rocks that prevail both up-stream and down, and with the islands less frequent. It shimmered in the light of a newborn sun; close ashore scarce a ripple stirred; but, despite its clear course and the beauty of its shining surface, I could see, a few yards out, the swirl of vicious eddies and marked the deadly speed of its major current, of all of which I was destined to have experience and to spare in times to come.

" Sir," I cried, " you cannot swim that! "

" Sir," says he, smiling again, " I shall not try."

Again he offered me his hand, and I wrung it. He ad barred further questioning, and he was going away. I felt that I bade good-bye to my last hope of escape from servitude, yet I would not show too much feeling, and mumbled I know not what words of adieux.

" Don't follow to the shore," he concluded, " for there may be a bare spice of danger there—and, if a sinful man's blessing does no harm, why," says he, looking me

135

full in the eyes with a tenderness in his handsome face that I could see he was half ashamed of—"why, God bless you, boy!"

To mock his sentiment, he made a prodigious flourish with his plumed hat, loosed his sword in its scabbard and, as if he were bound for a royal levée, strode down the terraces that sloped right to the river's edge. The house concealed him from the highroad, and this was well, for he had not made much of his jaunty progress along a way that was patently none too familiar to him when I heard the commotion of the posse's arrival at "Lynton" gate.

Horses neighed; men shouted, hailing the house; and some foolish body—most like that half-breed, Sam Chance—discharged a pistol.

"Ho, Master Ranger!" they chorused.—"Ho, Master Scull!" And: "Here we be, Master Scull— has the bird flown?"

Hidden from them just now, but a fair mark so soon as anyone bethought him to round the building, my annoying Stranger scorned to quicken his pace. To my troubled eyes, he seemed to walk as slowly as he could.

But "Lynton,"—through supposing its confiding guest at ease, if it had slept hard and long after its exciting evening,—woke, at the summons, into noisy life. The whole household roused itself as one man. Feet hammered to and fro. Voices called; doors banged. The outside servants fell pell-mell from their shanties and ran, half-clad, in the direction of the arrivals. I heard a front window thrown up with careless clamor and, riding clear of all the fracas, my uncle's high voice in a strident order:

"Surround the place! Surround the place! He sleeps in the west-wing!"

"Does he yet?" demanded the keen tones of the Constable of Hempfield. "Find first the messenger you sent us, for I'll lay the pair of 'em's made off together!"

At that, which could not have reached the chief object of their quest, the hullabaloo redoubled and I, sliding into a thicket that descended to the water, disregarded the Stranger's warning and stole to the river's lip to make reconnaissance of how things should fare there. I was no sooner at my destination and screened by a leafy barricade than the noises above convinced me of the flight's discovery, and a party of searchers came running around the house.

The Stranger stood at the shore now and would not turn. He gave three sharp whistles. From almost at my feet a boat put out, the oars manned by an athletic looking fellow with curling hair, who drew up to the unconcerned fugitive.

"Is all well, Harley?" I heard the Stranger ask.

"All's well, zur."

"Scull's boats?"

"All zeen to, zur."

The pursuit was plunging down the hill. Peeping out incautiously, I saw them come: Jones in the lead, afoot—for the posse had dismounted on its arrival; that practised bloodhound, the grinning Little Jacob, abreast of him and Chance; fat Cartlidge puffing in the rear; but nightgowned old Simon, for all his age, but two paces behind the Constable and in one of his perfect fits of courage. All save the Ranger bore guns.

The Stranger leapt aboard the boat. The man whom he addressed as Harley shoved off and pushed into the swirling current.

" Sit down, zur! " I heard him implore.

The Stranger shrugged and remained erect in the unsteady skiff.

The posse brought up at the water just in time to save themselves a ducking. Little Jacob fired and missed.

" Boats! " shouted Jones. " Get him alive! Where are your boats, Ranger? "

Harley labored manfully at his oars. Each instant saw the skiff widen that strip of water which lay betwixt it and the shore.

Uncle Simon hopped up and down, his peaked nightcap bobbing, his shift fluttering in the cold morning breeze. I could only suppose that he had remained in his nightclothes to retain to the end the appearance of good faith toward his guest, but he bothered with no false pretenses now.

" Boats? " he screeched.   Across current and through
eddy, the skiff was making certain way, the Stranger
upright in its stern, his back toward the shore.   " Never
mind boats: shoot him while you can! "

Little Jacob was reloading, but the Constable's posse
hesitated between conflicting orders.

" The reward's bigger if we get him alive," argued
the canny Cartlidge, and Constable Jones nodded
strong agreement.

Red-haired Patterson and Daunt his servant had
begun to rummage in the bushes on the other side of the
lawn from my hiding-place.   Little Jacob lowered his
piece and drew the Ranger behind his giant form.

" Man in boat might hit Master," he grunted, and I
could have sworn there was in that face, which custom-
arily evinced fear of my uncle, as much of affection as
such a countenance was capable of.

But Simon Scull sprang forward again and let out
a startling oath.

" Shoot him! " he yelled.   The Susquehannock shot
a second time.   He had craftily singled out the oarsman, and he nearly winged him.

" The other man! " commanded Uncle Simon.
" Never mind the servant.   Will nobody kill the other
man for me? "

His own skinny hands snatched the yellow-haired
Constable's rifle.   It flew to his shoulder.   I all but
cried a warning to the Stranger, but a word from his

oarsman—I could see it uttered, but could not hear it —served that turn. The fugitive looked over his shoulder. He was laughing!

"Be careful, Ranger!" he called.

Uncle Simon swore and shot. He was not, I know, unskilled with firearms, but rage is a poor marksman: his bullet went wild, and he threw down the gun. Thrifty Jones bent to recover it.

The Stranger flung off his cloak. He held a pistol in either hand. The weapon in his right barked: the Constable's rifle-butt was shattered. The left-held pistol spurted flame, and a black hole showed in the high peak of Uncle Simon's nightcap.

"So much for a warning!" laughed the Stranger.

Then he sat him down and shipped a second pair of oars.

Knowles Daunt ran up.

"We've f'und t'boats," he reported, "but they're all stove in, sir."

I looked at the skiff, and, as I looked, it leaped onward and onward toward the York County shore. It had two to drive it now. Another shot and another sought it. I thought that one might have hit the Stranger, but he did not slacken his stroke, and the skiff was soon out of range.

It began to appear to me that I had now better give some thought to my own predicament. I had seen enough to guess that it was perilously precarious.

CHAPTER XVIII

INDIAN GUILE

WELL, I reflected, there must still be some chance left me, if nothing could be proved. After all, what the Constable could produce was mere suspicion of my course. I had somewhat amazingly hurried from the jail, it was true, but I had first delivered my message, and the manner of my going might be only a boyish prank. Here at " Lynton," nobody had seen me in communication with the Stranger: it was just possible that none might ask hard questions. What if I now returned quietly to my room and there waited the issue of events?

To do less were to neglect the sole chance of escaping detection. I troubled myself not a little as to whether any of the parting shots had come home to my benefactor, but that was past help, and no immediate pursuit was possible. I resolved to make the safest use of my opportunity.

Stealthily, I worked back throught the bushes, the way that I had come; but I no sooner reached the level of the house than I remembered my loyal stallion. Gratitude and policy alike demanded a search for him: I boldly crossed the wood.

THE RANGER OF THE SUSQUEHANNOCK

To my joy, there was faithful Success standing exactly as I had left him. A peep toward the stable discovered that part of the yard deserted, the Shawanese having crept by devious routes to the riverside to watch events there; I got my good animal into his stall, made him a comfortable if hurried bed, saw to water and food for him and then made again for the house, of which the front door had been left standing wide in the excitement of the chase.

I stole through the empty hall, through the empty dining-room. I passed into the kitchen. But the kitchen was not empty: I had forgotten the giantess Massáya!

I stopped short in my tracks.

Her broad back was toward me, and the upper half invisible: she was leaning out of a window that must give view of the river. Was her attention entirely engrossed by what she watched? Would it be barely possible to creep by her unheard? I could but try.

Infinitely cautious, I tiptoed into that room. In a second, I was half-way to my own and safety.

Was the thing all a trap? It may have been; I had heard much of Indian guile and have since seen some of it at work. Perhaps her crafty husband, guessing what lay behind the Stranger's exit from "Lynton" had, even in the confusion of awaking, set her in wait for me; perhaps, honestly engaged in seeing what she could of the activities by the river, she had nevertheless

142

heard my approach through the house, understood it and retained her seemingly unconscious posture the better to lay me at last by the heels. In any case, deeply though she had slept through the preceding night, the squaw must have possessed ears between her shoulders: she turned—saw me—charged.

She did not cry out, nor, I think, did I. The situation left no breath for words. Even in their most pressing need, large people move, as a rule, somewhat slowly: Massáya, her snake-locks streaming, came at me like a thunder-bolt.

Back I wheeled, as a cockroach darts from sudden light. I scuttled for the dining-room, reached its door and was closing that on my retreat when she got to it.

Then she had me. In such an immense grasp, struggle was useless, yet instinct fought her, and in a terrible silence Massáya fought. I bit; I scratched. She fetched me clout after clout. I staggered, and she enfolded me in the bone-crushing embrace of a sovereign bear. It was over: she dragged me to my cell and threw me on its pallet-bed. She was not even breathing hard as she walked away. She closed its portal, and I heard the boards creak as she leaned against them, outside, on guard.

I ran to the window, but there was thence no escape: the disgruntled posse was returning to the lawn. Patterson's brogue uttered hard complaints; Cartlidge wheezed threats, and the sharp tones of the Constable were vowing that he would even yet secure the reward. I waited for my uncle to dismiss them as a criminal condemned waits the voice of the hangman.

It happened at a long last; they were given ale, which they consumed greedily, yet grumblingly, and finally rode off. Then the shambling step of Uncle Simon and his steward's soft tread came into the kitchen; Massáya addressed to them a brief sentence that escaped me, and the pair entered where I crouched.

Somehow, it was my uncle I now feared the more. Little Jacob turned his horrid grin on me and rolled his blind eye; but the face of his master was terrible with an icy rage. Even from his pimples the blood had retreated, and he was a grisly white. Under his vulturine nose, his mouth worked; his glance was like chilled steel. It was all the worse because, when he did speak, he used the Quaker forms: that he had himself in perfect control lent the more deadliness to his sinister determination.

" So thee's here at last," said he.

I rose. I could not help trembling in body, but my spirit I mastered. I bowed assent.

Little Jacob looked at my uncle and grinned in a devilish mixture of love and fear and admiration. The Ranger had eyes for me alone.

" Thee stands on a precipice-brink," he said. " I am master here at ' Lynton '—master of life and death— and I tolerate no traitors in my house. Have a care, boy, and answer: Did thee warn this felon that has just escaped us? "

Conscience is the strangest of man's qualities. Last night, when there might have been some doubt of the results, I had equivocated in replying to Uncle Simon's inquisition as to how much I had observed in the attic-room; yet now, when denial might have had an equal chance of belief, and when the consequences of truth were plainly indicated as fatal, I had not even thought of lying. Approaching the house, I had planned mendacity; Massáya's capture could, of itself, prove nothing: I would not pursue the road that that suggested. My next words might be my last, but false they would not be.

" I have to tell you that I warned your guest," said I.

" Ah! " cried the Ranger, and stretched out his arms at me like the arms of a gorilla. The long fingers spread and curled.

Little Jacob touched him and made what I took to be an offer to do for his master this violence which that master contemplated. With a snarl, Uncle Simon shook off the Indian's hand; he did not even turn his head from me. His eyes were red again. Slowly he advanced.

" And," said I, " if that likes you, why last night I saw what it was that you put into your strong-box."

Uncle Simon rushed.

THE RANGER OF THE SUSQUEHANNOCK

I flung up arms that I knew would be impotent against two tormentors. The Stranger had said: "We can always fight before arrest." I would fight for my life, even though I knew the fight to be hopeless.

CHAPTER XIX

PINNED TO THE MATTRESS

HERE in our new country, we think it no shame to be as God made us; even such boys as my dear grandsons learn early to practice those weapons of offence and defence that the Almighty has furnished as a part of the natural body of each; but only two generations ago in England, this was accounted no art for a gentleman. During my early days, lads of family were made familiar with their swords, but not with their fists; we could employ firearms, but our own arms of bone and muscle we knew not how to use alone. It was an error of pride for which many paid dear, and in this crisis it bade fair to render me a heavy score.

I struck out blindly and with both hands. Uncle Simon knew no more of these matters than did I, but he had a lean toughness acquired from his rough life, and he had the rage of madness. Last night I had been the stronger, but last night had worn me out. His thin arms were like flails. They beat down mine. They fell upon my unguarded face, and I, in turn, fell under them. I slipped to the floor beside the bed, and the Ranger bent dreadfully over me to complete my punishment.

Help came from an unexpected quarter. Little Jacob was rocking himself to and fro in an ecstasy of delight, ready to assist in the punishment were he needed and scarcely able to check the impulse to volunteer; but through the window lithe forms hurtled, and Uncle Simon paused to look up at Iron Hatchet and Billy, whose admiration I had won when I mastered Success, and whose gratitude I had secured by my handclasp after their own torturing in Philadelphia.

"How now?" cried my uncle. One hand rested on my chest, the other was raised to strike.

Little Jacob advanced toward the intruders.

"Wait!" The Ranger's caution was returning; he stayed his steward.

The Shawanese were in considerable terror, which made their action the more commendable. They offered no physical impediment, but began to chatter, both at once, in their own tongue, something clearly intended to suspend the outrage.

"Talk English!" Uncle Simon commanded. He spoke several of the native dialects, but Shawanese he had never mastered.

Obedient to his order, the servants broke into an English explanation that was for a time equally unintelligible and that I now believe to have been a tissue of well-intended falsehoods. We made out finally that they, while on some employ at the front of the house, had heard our noise and achieved this quick entrance because they guessed its nature and possessed news which, in their master's interest, should prevent it. They said that some red servants, happening over from " Hempfield," had told how Mr. Wright liked not my uncle's attitude toward me, as revealed on our journey together, and expressed himself as meaning to keep me in his eye: if I came by any ill at my uncle's hands, the Magistrate would surely make legal inquiry.

I say I do not now believe this. Nevertheless, Uncle Simon had a countryside reputation for severity; it was upon his harshness that his value as Ranger of the Manor partly depended. Without doubt he knew this; moreover, he was doing a wrong, and those who do wrong open a gate to fear. He glowered at the intruders.

"Go away," he said, and pointed to the window.

Little Jacob aped his gesture.

The poor souls of Shawanese had done what they could. They slunk off.

For my part, I was too sick with my beating to raise my head. Uncle Simon bent his above it. His face was nothing pleasant to contemplate.

"There be joost enough sense in what t'fools say," he declared, " t'mak' me let oop for this once. Think not this affair is at an end, nephew. By t'time we got whole boats, that gallant was lost in t'woods on t'other side, and there was nawt to follow; but the fellow will be caught yet. So be you well warned "—his eyes burned into me—"if ever word is breathed about what was seen in t'attic, if 'tis proved my own bond-boy gave warning to yon highwayman, that will hap whereby my nephew will mak' no trouble more at ' Lynton ' ! " He gave me a kick in the ribs. " Now thee shall get up," he concluded, regaining his Quaker speech, " and do a day's work—and see to it thee holds thy tongue! "

I tried to rise, but toppled over on the bed.

" I can't! " I moaned, too bruised to budge.

" Little Jacob make him," suggested the Susquehannock, his sinister blind eye heaving blankly.

But Uncle Simon was all caution now. " No," says he; " it might look ill, and this escape will bring folk about. Thee may rest here to-day," he added to me, " but 'twill be the last rest thee'll get. Jacob, see that he doesn't show himself to any visitors."

With that, he turned on his heel and shuffled out. The steward grinned at me.

" Boy safe now," he said, " but this heap rough country. Heap many accidents." And he also passed from the room.

It was plain enough to me that I stood in grave danger, and yet I was for hours so sick that I scarce cared. All the rest of that morning, I lay on my pallet in a kind of lethargy. At noon, Massáya grudgingly brought me some broth, but I was little better when, at twilight, she came in with a scanty evening meal. It grew very cold as night fell, so variable is our weather in these parts, and so quickly does the winter often follow on our Indian Summer's heels; there were no blankets to cover me, and I lay through dragging hours of darkness, and the same sounds as on the preceding night, now shivering until my teeth chattered, and anon burning with fever.

Some good the food must, however, have wrought in me—or else my inherited strength of constitution and that buoyancy which is nearly every lad's served me well—for I did at length mend enough to consider my situation.   Long I lay revolving it in my troubled mind.

The Susquehannock was a murderer; his worst I might, of course, avoid; but what was I to make of my uncle? His rage there was no denying, yet I could not think him disposed, in his cooler moments, to go so far as his cruel steward. My lot would be hard, if I remained here; but it should not be death if I kept a watch on Little Jacob and held my tongue about those jewels. They would not down in my memory, nor would Uncle Simon's treachery to his guest, about which I had had scant opportunity to make inquiry of that host and concerning which he had, of course, vouchsafed not a syllable. Whether the Stranger was indeed acting in my father's behalf, there had been no time to demand of him, as there had been none to tell him who I was or ask his own identity: he seemed a daring man quite capable of employing any ruse for his own purpose. I went over and over everything that I could recall from my childhood, seeking to find a clue to my uncle's animosity toward me: I was but a boy, and I found none. Perhaps he was only a miser. My Rowntree pride still bade adherence to my promise, and the neighborhood of Magistrate Wright lent some hope of refuge should matters turn to the worst.

About and about, my mind swam like a rat in a bucket. Now I would plan to run away; then I would ask myself whither I could go and how, if I went to "Hempfield," I could support my story of abuse against the certainly combined testimony of my uncle and his steward. Again I would argue that my indenturing must be illegal, and at once felt sure it must be as legal as it was unjust. And always, at the completion of the circle—so soon as to be again begun—there was the dark angel of my pride in a pledged word.

The cold settled deeper and deeper, and a bright moon shone. At last I determined to bear my burthen, to watch Little Jacob and to do my seeming duty unless or until I made sure that that seeming was false. Only then, still fully dressed, did I fall into a troubled sleep, waking now and again to suffer from the frigidity of the weather—to start as some mouse scraped in the wall —some wind rattled at the pane—or some board creaked in the house. It must have been nigh morning ere I slept.

Sounds and smells of breakfast-getting in the kitchen

awakened me. A cold sun was beating at the heavily frosted window, and, scratching away the rime, I looked across a lawn white with hoar-frost to a woodland almost wintry. I turned at sound of approaching footsteps and realized that Massáya or her husband was bringing me food.

The door was swung open with the slowness of one who bears a tray. I did not want to seem too far recovered and so made for my bed again and, in so doing, saw something that had escaped me in the hurry of my rising.

A piece of paper was pinned to the makeshift mattress. Instinctively, I hid it inside my jacket.

The squaw came in, carrying food. She stared at me, and I wondered if she guessed my secret, but she said not so much as " Good Morning," and I durst as yet venture on no speech with her. I waited until she was gone and then, leaning against the door, took out the paper.

It was a letter. Somebody had entered the cell while I lay in my stupor. I read:

" To the Brave Lad at ' Lynton.'

" *Honored Sir:*
  " This I send with my servant, lest it prove unduly perilous to wake you and give the message by word of mouth. Though, in the haste of my regretful departure, I made some opportunity to thank you for your timely assistance, yet I could not then (arrange-

ments being incompleted) tell that of which I now
hasten to inform you; to wit, sir, that should your sense
of honor (which God forbid I should attempt to inveigle) ever permit a change in your resolution to remain at 'Lynton,' or should danger to you there at
once demand aid and yet provide sufficient warning to
make the plan possible, you may find a friend in this
manner following:

"On any day before ten o' the clock in the morning,
sir, cross, alone, to the west bank of the Susquehanna
at Wright's Ferry and follow the York Highroad until
you shall have come to its junction with the trail leading back to that other ferry, called Anderson's; pursue
this trail to the first roadside spring, which is close beside the foot of the forest-covered hill known as Round
Top. Over against this spring stands a dead and
forked black-oak; put a freshly-broken branch in the
fork of the oak; then go your way and return, again
alone, an hour before noonday. More than this may
not at the present writing be said; but I add again my
hearty thanks to you, and the admiration, sir, of

"Your Honor's most Obt. Svt.,
"The Gentleman Whom Your Honor Rescued."

Hastily I restored this odd letter to its hiding-place
in my jacket. I could not doubt the authorship; its
curious mingling of sincere gratitude and goodwill with
a half-mocking treatment of me, was what I should
have expected from my intercourse with the Stranger,
and the first feeling that it produced was one of pure
joy, not only for his apparently safe escape, but, I

154

fear, more for this assurance that I was not wholly helpless.

Soon, however, these feelings were replaced by some that did me no credit whatever. The unfortunate are fair prey for selfishness and the bitterness of recrimination. It was, I reflected, all very fine for this man in his freedom to offer me aid; but how was I to avail myself of it? When there arose (as it seemed there soon must) some crisis in my affairs, it would come with little chance of my crossing that wild river to seek a champion; and, even if the chance offered, how was I, a stranger myself in this wilderness, to find my way to the trysting-place?

I upbraided myself for my ingratitude, but the ingratitude persisted, and presently—since ingratitude ever drags suspicion in its train—I asked myself another question:

Cruel as my uncle was, he need not be a liar in all things. Constable Jones had said that the Maryland outlaw had ere this visited Europe. I had no genuine proof of the fugitive's identity. How could I know indeed that the Stranger, a revealed highwayman, was not in very truth the renegade Cresap?

CHAPTER XX

THE RANGINGS OF THE RANGER

WHILE it was still very early in the morning, Uncle Simon came to my room and displayed again an evidence of what I can call only his crafty daring. He told me that, as Ranger of the Manor, it lay in the course of his duty to make written reports of disturbances such as yesterday's and submit it to Mr. Wright in the latter's character of District-Magistrate; that, during the night, he had accomplished his account of the highwayman's escape, omitting as a kindness to me—so he said—all mention of my part therein, and that this was now about to be dispatched to " Hempfield " by the hand of Iron Hatchet.

" And," says he, looking narrowly at me, " thee shall ride with him."

His purpose, of course, in withholding denunciation of my aid to the Stranger was evident enough: he wanted to balance my knowledge of those mysterious jewels by his knowledge of my assistance to a criminal. Yet his intent in sending me to the Wright plantation was something of the most hidden. A flush of surprise must have betrayed the emotion it aroused, for he smiled sourly and added:

" Oh, thee can work no wickedness against me! There is nawt thee can tell the Magistrate, and nowhere for thee to go, and Iron Hatchet, though he may love thee, loves his life more. Thee's heard that John Wright fears harm for thee. Very well: he shall see with his own eyes that none has befallen—but remember what I have said, that harm enough will hap if thee say one word of that on which I have commanded silence."

So it was that, bruised as I still was, I rode to " Hempfield " for the first time. Swifts circled above the chimneys of " Lynton " when we left it; the sun hung like a big medal low in the clear east, and as we rode, the brisk air, with its touch of winter, raised my spirits, and I thought to gain from my companion some of the information for which my curiosity so loudly clamored.

That hope went, however, unsatisfied. Iron Hatchet was in plain terror of his master, and it was speedily clear that I might as yet expect from him no more than he had already done. Indeed, he vowed that his interference when Uncle Simon attacked me was only what he had represented it to the Ranger, and all the use I could make of him was to get him to point out Round Top, which, once indicated, proved an unmistakable hill, the highest among those rising abruptly from the river north of the ferry.

This and one thing more: he said that, though the

boats had been repaired at " Lynton," and others could be procured from near-by plantations, pursuit of the Stranger was suspended until a larger force could be gathered together, the posse of yesterday counting itself, despite Jones's urgings, as too small in number to brave the York County woods.

We did not go so far along the highroad as the corner where Mr. Wright had left us on the evening of the Ranger's home-coming, but turned, instead, into a scarcely observable trail, which right soon opened into a sort of avenue lined with cultivated trees: cherry-trees they were, and the road was that which you know as Cherry Lane, where the settlers from the Palatinate now celebrate their annual festival. From this the long, narrow walls of gray " Hempfield House " came hospitably into view, with quiet hop-fields beyond them, and I began to wonder whether, after all, I might not find some means of securing a promise of protection from the Magistrate.

Therein also I was disappointed. Mr. Wright, so an Indian servant named Prince informed us, was from home, and we could but leave the Ranger's report in this man's keeping. I was for demanding some member of the family, but it seemed that the Magistrate's daughter, Mistress Susannah, who managed his estate, was a person of some exclusiveness and would see nobody unnecessarily, nor permit others of the family so to do. Thus I failed, at this juncture, to meet a lady who was the correspondent of Mr. Pope, the poet, in England, the friend of Mr. Franklin in Philadelphia, and the first importer of silkworms in America.

This would have meant little to me then, but one piece of information we were given by which my fortunes were to be immediately affected. That lazy Hempfield Indian had been about to ride to "Lynton," on a mission from Mr. Wright; now we should execute it. We were to tell my uncle that another friendly redskin had brought word that Cresap, or at least some of his fellows, had lately been using, and might even now be making use of, a certain long deserted and lonely cabin near the Joppa Trail, on the west bank of the Susquehanna, where it was thought that some of their private memoranda were secretly stored. The revengeful Patterson would shortly send his servant, Knowles Daunt, to reconnoitre, and if Daunt found the news correct, he was to return with all speed, raise a large force and go back with it to arrest the outlaw: Patterson wished to omit Jones and Cartlidge from the expedition, because they argued for a small band and consequent larger shares of the reward, but the Ranger was to be summoned, and Mr. Wright suggested his sending word to Jones at Lancaster in order to make the attack the legal proceeding that it ought to be.

It was this information that we brought home to Uncle Simon, and you may surmise with what mixed emotions I heard Iron Hatchet deliver it. If the man hiding in that lonely cabin on the Joppa Trail, wherever that might be, were somebody other than the Stranger, then I could be on the side of the law, but if he were my benefactor, why I did not want him taken!

Again I reproached myself for my bitter thoughts of him. I listened to Iron Hatchet with a sinking heart.

Uncle Simon was, however, a man of action. He started at the first words of the Shawanese. Then— he had met us at the gate—he turned toward the house and called:

" Jacob!—Little Jacob! "

The huge Susquehannock came out of the front door and ran lightly toward us. My uncle took a few steps to meet him and said something that I did not alto- gether catch; but the conclusion of it rang clear:

" Ride at once to Lancaster and find the Constable. "

He ordered me to stable Success and Iron Hatchet's mount and thereafter help Massáya in the kitchen. These commands given, he hurried indoors and up- stairs.

Still too sore to make haste without supervision, I was yet in the stable when Little Jacob entered and, sneeringly pretending disregard of me, saddled and led out his own horse and rode away. Now, that stable stood on " Lynton's " right. From some thirty paces, it faced the kitchen, through the open door whereof the vast Massáya was visible, moving about her domestic tasks and looking, doubtless under instructions, ever and again at me; but it also commanded a partial view of the lawn directly before the house, and upon this portion of the lawn I presently saw Uncle Simon issue.

He glanced furtively about, but the shadows of the stable hid me. He saw nobody, yet so careful did he seem not to be himself observed that I pressed tight against the door-jamb and, risking detection by Massáya, watched his every move.

The cool sunlight fell on a brace of pistols in his belt. He was dressed for a journey, and yet, so far as I had heard, no horse was ordered for him. During one moment, I expected him to come to the stable to prepare his own mount, but the next I noted that he wore stout walking-boots and that he carried a thick staff. Once more he glanced in all directions; he satisfied himself that the grounds were deserted; and immediately disappeared around the west wing. Before I could move, I heard him run down the terraces at the back of the house and toward the river.

Something secret was afoot. I determined to find out what it was.

That was my instantaneous resolve. I still ached from my beating; I had incurred the enmity of all this household; I had recently been severely threatened as to the consequences of future offending, and yet here I was keen to deserve them. Well, that is what it is to be a boy with a boy's courageous curiosity. I told myself that I would not be forever fubbed off with lies, or half-truths, or suppressions—that perhaps my father's name had not been falsely introduced among these mysteries—that the Stranger might be in peril—and that my own plight might be bettered if I knew too much rather than too little. So I edged through the door.

"You come in help!"

Masdáya leaned out of the kitchen, her face ominous.

"I have not finished here," I answered truly.

"You hurry," she growled and stood resolutely, strong arms akimbo, watching the stable.

There was no escape in that direction. I plunged into the shadows of the interior and saw, cutting them, a ray of light above the stall of brave Success. Here was a high window, as I now remembered, looking away from the house. I patted my stallion.

"Stand quiet, Success!" I whispered.

He did. I got upon his back and reached the sill. He stood without movement or sound while I drew myself erect. I raised the sash, pulled myself up, straddled the sill and dropped to the ground.

Luck was with me. A low hedge ran from the nearest corner of the barn all the way down the terrace's border to the river-shore and so furnished a screen betwixt me and the kitchen. Along the south side of this I ran, crouching, to the very rim of the water. As I stuck my head through the bushes there, I saw Uncle Simon in midstream, alone in one of his repaired skiffs and pulling hard for the farther bank.

THE RANGINGS OF THE RANGER

It would not do to follow so long as he could see me; it would not very well do to remain here after Massáya had—as she soon must—missed me up the hill, yet that was my alternative. If I got a boat and pushed off, Uncle Simon, rowing for the York County side and so facing home, must assuredly observe my pursuit and balk my espionage, perhaps with physical violence; if, on the other hand, Massáya caught me on the grounds, she might be persuaded that I was merely exploring my new surroundings and certainly would suspend the climax of punishment until my uncle's return: of the pair of evils I chose the lesser and lay quiet.

I escaped both. Uncle Simon landed on the other side at a spot I could identify by a lonely, sharp rock that rose there, and Massáya seemed not yet to have gone to the stable to hurry me. As soon as I made sure the Ranger must have turned into the forest, I ran, sore as I was, into the open and sought the other boats at that place at which they had yesterday been found.

They were all there, and most of them in very fair condition again. Having had a little experience of such matters at home, both on Derwent-water and in the coves along our shore of North Sea coast, I called on that hurriedly to select the best and had just begun to shove off when I heard a mighty voice bellowing from the terraces above.

"Where you go?—You come back!"

It was Massáya, and at the sound of her my lungs

collapsed like an emptied bagpipe. I could see her fairly. Her short skirts were no impediment to her advance: she was running toward the shore.

By desperate effort, I regained some breath and scrambled to the other boats. I collected their oars and flung them into my chosen skiff. Now she could not follow. If she was armed, of course ——

" Massáya kill! "

She was within fifty yards now. I gave my boat a great push and jumped in. I shipped my oars and plied them for dear life. Already I was out of reach, but I was far from being out of pistol-range.

She had to come to the shore. The water lapped her moccasins. Her face was hideous with rage. She raised a hand.

Yes, if she were armed, she could make good her threat, and I had small doubt but that she would try. Yet still my luck held; she had come away too suddenly upon her discovery, and so had come weaponless. Pulling with my head between my knees, I saw her run from oarless boat to oarless boat, and then I knew that, until I met whatever new dangers lurked on the river's farther side, I was safe.

CHAPTER XXI

IN COLD BLOOD

THERE are some respects wherein, it seems to me, our Colonials have softened. Nowadays, unless he be a farmhand or a soldier, a man in this part of Pennsylvania sometimes lies abed as late as seven o'clock. Not so was it when first I came here. Except we had been up all the night, master and servant alike rose with dawn, more often long before it, and so you are to understand that it was still very early morning when my skiff grated on the pebbles of the York County shore, behind the lonely rock that I had marked, and I pulled it up beside Uncle Simon's boat, which, as I expected, lay beached there.

The thicket of willows at the water's edge had been disturbed in one place only, so that a clear trail was furnished me. At first my fear was lest the Ranger should be close by, and so I proceeded among the reeds and underbrush with caution; but soon the clue brought me to a more open way, and there I learned that Uncle Simon's business was at some distance.

A path ran up direct to the thicket's wall and stopped —or, if you prefer, began—at that. It had not been recently used, so, in the swamp-ground close to the

165

water, the tangle of brush had overgrown it; but once firm land was reached, growth was slower: it showed plain enough and, as it ran straight inland only (and as there were no further tokens of torn leaf or broken twig to say that its latest traveller had turned aside) I saw that Uncle Simon must have taken this course. The path, though walled with green, lay clear enough for the first hundred yards; nobody was visible: I could start forward with small chance of detection.

For the second time this morning, my spirits rose. It was that strange moment of our Pennsylvania year when winter peeps in at one door and midsummer looks back through the other. A half-dozen sorts of birds flashed their brilliant plumage close beside me, or sang their songs almost in my ear, and this although the foliage, under touch of last night's early frost, was already donning its deeper colors of autumn. Youth was curing my bruises and adventure obliterating the memory of them; I had outwitted Massáya; mystery lurked ahead of me for my solving. I gave no thought to the difficulties of explanation that beset return to "Lynton": for an hour or two, I should be free; the day was young, and so was I.

Nevertheless, an instinct for some degree of wariness did not forsake me. While my breath held, I ran softly and at every turn of the path paused, crouched and made vigilant reconnaissance. Perhaps three miles had thus been covered when I came in sight of my uncle.

IN COLD BLOOD

He was ambling ahead, not hurriedly, yet with an even speed. His back was toward me; his shoulders were stooped, but his right hand, which held the walking-stick, swung it with a fine vigor. On the whole, Uncle Simon seemed to be enjoying his promenade as thoroughly as I was enjoying mine.

I stopped and let him gain on me. I waited until a twist of the way hid him again. Then I went on forward.

But when I, too, reached the next turn, I halted abruptly.

A small clearing lay ahead, roughly circular and perhaps fifty feet in diameter. Save where the thin track entered and left it, the forest grew tight around, and in the centre stood a one-room log-cabin, badly weathered, but with a brand-new door of considerable apparent strength, fresh boards nailed across the windows and loopholes, as if for guns, recently hacked through the stubborn walls.

Only a few yards from the circle's edge, Uncle Simon had come to a dead stop. His cane had been transferred to his left hand, and in his right he held a cocked pistol. He was studying the hut as if his eyes could bore through its walls and tell him whether or no someone hid within.

I ducked a few feet aside behind a thick chestnut and noiselessly dropped flat on the mossy turf. The act was timely!

Uncle Simon quietly turned his scrutiny elsewhere. By keeping my belly tight to the earth and just raising my face, I could watch him well.

First he stood there like a statue, but all ears, and I thanked Heaven that my fall had been a silent one. Then he sprang alive with catlike action. His red eyes, having devoured the hut, swept the entire circle, and I drew my head down as if his glance were his pistol. When I dared look slowly up again, he was making a nimble tour of the clearing, his weapon alert, one thin finger on its trigger. He ran down the exit of the path and straightway back again. He came thence across to its entrance and gazed over the trail that we had both lately travelled: he was so close to me that I could have touched him by the mere stretching-out of my hand.

This last deed of observation seemed to satisfy him. He legged it to the log-hut.

Of course I know now every foot of all this countryside. I know that what we had followed, like beast and hunter, was the old Joppa Trail, which saved some distance between the river and the Joppa Road that runs south from the town of York. I know, too, that at this time of my introduction to it, the trail had been long deserted for a still shorter cut. However, though on that crisp morning I could only give a guess to such matters, I made this conjecture:

Here must be the house Cresap had been reported

168

as using. My uncle's avarice had driven him into one of his fits of desperate courage: he was come alone to make the arrest and secure for himself the total reward!

Already he was at the door of the hut.

Would he be killed? Not alone, for unarmed as I was and dislike him and distrust him as I even then did, yet must I help so long as he was my master and I his debtor.

I got to my feet. Even as I realized that duty, one other thought flashed through my startled brain: assist my uncle I must, but—let death itself be the price—I would not harm the Stranger. Should he be inside that hut and so, by his presence, prove himself Cresap, I should yet do what was possible to further his escape.

My foot was raised to run forward. There it was arrested by what I saw.

My uncle took a huge key from the pocket of his bulging brown coat. He inserted it in the lock of the new door and entered the hut like a man come home.

What could it mean?

As I put the question, I told myself that it was folly to pretend or doubt. I recalled the complaints that all the Pennsylvanians' plans were revealed, in advance of attempted execution, to the Marylanders. Here was the explanation: the Ranger of the Manor—my uncle! —sold his official secrets to Thomas Cresap.

One comfort came like music: If the Stranger were Cresap, Uncle Simon might have been playing fast and loose with both sides and, now that yesterday morning's happenings had revealed an endeavor to sell his guest, he might have decided to retrieve his honor by killing the fugitive. That course would cover his treachery to Thomas Penn and, at the same time, secure the lesser reward that was offered for the dead body of the outlaw.

But this was too fantastic: the Ranger had his own sort of bravery, yet, from what I had seen of him in the presence of that uninvited guest, I made sure it would not extend to tracking him down alone in these woods which were haunted by his retainers. No, said I to myself, wherever the Stranger was and whoever he was, he was not expected here, and he was not Cresap.

Then I noticed another thing: Uncle Simon did not close the door after him; he left it hanging ajar. It rocked gently in a light breeze, and this gave the place an air of utter desertion.

To the day of my death, I shall blame myself for my inaction during what followed. I was a bright lad and vain of my wit, and yet, what was no excuse, my bewilderment beclouded the intention of that swinging door.

For I drew back to cover and began to seek some less discreditable accounting of my relative's conduct. Spies are ever ill-paid: why should a man whose estates in Pennsylvania were endangered by the Marylanders, a man of Uncle Simon's position, wreck his honor and risk his life for the paltry sums that must be all he would receive in return for his information? Whatever the defects of Simon Scull's character, a weakness for poor bargain was not among them. And where, if, despite that, this man were at once such a traitor and such a short-sighted creature—where did my boasted sense of duty lead me now? Where——

Not for the nonce, at least, were those inquiries to be answered. While the framing of them bent my head to my breast behind the chestnut, somebody else had stolen into the clearing.

I heard him at last and looked up.

It was Knowles Daunt, the honest, home-recalling north-countryman, who had been kind to me in the jail at Lancaster; the man, as I now recollected, whose master Patterson was to send him here to reconnoitre. He had clearly but just come up, and yet he was already half-way to the hut. That innocently swinging door had deceived him with its air of desertion: he held his rifle unreadily.

Perhaps I could not guess the baseness of the trap that lay so plain before me. I know that I did not cry out.

Then Uncle Simon leapt to the doorway. He held a pistol, and the pistol spurted flame.

CHAPTER XXII

JUSTICE TAKES THE TRAIL

I TURNED and ran.

No one, I venture, will say that I was a cowardly boy, or even a timid; rather has rashness always been my character, and in those days there was super-added that over-riding curiosity which is so often mistaken for courage in the young, an inquisitiveness that is at once a habit and a passion, stronger than either discretion or fear, and tyrannical enough to harness bravery to its chariot. But now had sprung at me, like a tiger from the jungle, something fiercer than my fiercest: I mean unexpected horror. Had there been more warning, I might have stood my ground; there was none: I ran.

Headlong I ran down the trail up which I had followed the Ranger. My first plunge must have been made while the explosion of his pistol, trebly loud in that confined clearing, deafened him to all other sound —while the smoke of the deed blinded him—for he had neither seen me nor heard, and I, no less insensate, rushed onward until I had covered a good quarter of the distance to the river. The birds fled before the

172

noise of my approach, the air that had been so bracing cut my lungs; all that was joyous had deserted that day. I ran until shortness of breath slowed my steps.

Reason returned only when action slackened. What was I to do?

Go back to Daunt's relief? But I was unarmed and should be helpless.

Go forward to "Lynton"? That would be to play into the Ranger's hand.

I bethought me of the letter that had been pinned to my pallet. I drew it out. At pause, I listened: the startled birds rustled behind their leafy screen; the alarming cry of what I now know must have been a wild turkey rose on the clear atmosphere and died away again, but there came no sound of any chase. I studied the Stranger's written directions:

" On any morning before ten of the clock ——"

Through a rift in the trees, the sun was shining. It must still be an hour's journey from ten.

" Alone ——"

Who could be more alone than such a fugitive as I was now?

" The west bank of the Susquehanna ——"

This was the west bank: the York County shore.

I made up my mind to find the trysting-place and set the signal.

It was no small task. Ingenuity it took and effort and, what was more precious, time. " Before ten " the

letter said it must be done. Clearly it was only at ten
o'clock that the Stranger visited some spot whence he
could observe the oak, yet Round Top, as Iron Hatchet
had pointed it out to me, stood well up the river from
my present position. To row my skiff as far as
Wright's Ferry would be perilous: Massáya might have
set a patrol on the water; yet it was doubtful if I could
find the way by land.

The attempt had to be made. It was necessary first
to gain the York Highroad, and that must make a
junction with the ferry-landing: as to this, one could
not go wrong if one followed the stream. I gained the
river's brink and headed north along it, but the banks
were steep; there was no trace of a trail, and every foot
of progress had to be fought for over rough ground and
through undergrowth that twined and tore and
whipped me.

It was done at last. The ferry-stage was just then
deserted, and the empty highroad stretched south from
it. I took to that and tramped it half a mile.

Then I again consulted the letter:

" Its junction with the trail leading back to that other
ferry, called Anderson's."

How was that trail to be recognized? Sign-post in
this wild valley there was none. Well, the trail was
made to connect with the highway; that was certain.
Therefore, it must be short. It would run so as to bring
travellers bound for York briefly to the more open road;

it would be one of the first trails I encountered. Some
chance had to be taken: I took the first.

The choice was right, and now my pilgrimage grew
facile. The path ran clear enough. I followed it
swiftly, looking to right and left for a spring and found
one when almost within sight of the river. Sure
enough, the gray peak of Round Top, towering high
over its cloak of dark pines like the head of some bird of
prey thrust up from its ruffled plumage, loomed close
ahead; across from the spring, the forest declined to
rushes that descended to the water, but in the midst of
it rose, so as to be notable from a long distance, a lonely
oak-tree, dead and bare of leaves; it had grown straight
above the rushes and then forked into a pair of now
skeleton arms.

I scrambled to its base and uprooted an entire bush,
its foliage turned a bright yellow by the frost. With
this buttoned into my jacket, I climbed the tree. I
placed the bush securely in the fork and returned to the
spring: if one were looking for it, from the blackened
oak that yellow thing would shine like a lanthorn.

But this little triumph had renewed my self-confi-
dence. The Stranger's letter indicated that he would
make no rendezvous until an hour short of noon. I
had an hour's space ahead of me and decided to employ
it by seeking news.

My thought was to go back to the ferry and spy
from cover on the ferrymen, when they made their next

trip over, in the hope of gathering some gossip from their talk; but when I reached the landing-stage it was to realize, what should have been easy to guess, that the boat ran only when there was someone to summon it. Travellers were few, and the boat was housed on the Lancaster County side: I could see it over there, a huge, flat thing, outlined against the white strip of road that cleft the forest to reach it; the pair of hands lay blanketed on its deck, sleeping, apparently, in the sun. It was a peevish boy that sat him down to wait a voyager.

As things were then in this disturbed district, I might have waited a week vainly, but the good fortune that had come to me in the earlier morning had not quite deserted. It could scarce have been ten minutes after my arrival when I, chilled and mighty hungry, saw a commotion at the farther landing-stage. Horsemen rode up, and the lazy hands sprang to their feet. The passengers came aboard, and the boat put off.

What alarm, if any, Massáya had given concerning my disappearance, it was bootless to conjecture. I was in the position of a runaway indentured-servant and quite outside the law. In these circumstances, there was no heart in me to court discovery, so I hid in the reeds a good fifteen yards from the landing-stage. But, as I peeped between the bushes yesterday at " Lynton," so I peeped now.

Slowly the boat, propelled by long poles in the hands

176

of Indian ferrymen, was worked across the river. I saw
the passengers standing by their horses: John Wright,
Crown Magistrate; the wiry Constable of Hempfield;
Sam Chance, the pudgy Cartledge, Patterson, the Irishman; Little Jacob and Billy and Iron Hatchet. All
carried rifles, and there, similarly armed, and holding
the bridle of his white mare and a perfect picture of
avenging Justice in quest of a criminal—Simon Scull
himself, the Ranger of the Manor!

I pulled my head into the bushes. I lay quiet. I
heard the boat grate against the landing-stage. There
was a confusion of cries and the rattle of hoofs. The
posse rode rapidly out the York Road.

Soon, however, with Simon Scull and the law thus
carried out of sight, my insatiable curiosity again grew
resurgent. I stole from my lurking-place among the
reeds. The lazy ferrymen had not been impressed for
police-duty; their part was to maintain a way for possible traffic, or a ready means of retreat in case the
expedition had sudden need of it. They were lolling on
the boat-deck, palpably ignorant Indians: I sauntered
up to them.

Whom they took me for I know not—perhaps some
farmhand from an outlying plantation, though almost
all men knew one another by sight in that sparsely-
settled countryside, and few wandered about alone on
foot. Be that as it may, I found the fellows eager to
talk: they had all the non-combatant's love for telling a

tale of war, and my questions begot ready answers. This is what I gathered from the broken English of those replies:

The posse of which I had been forewarned at " Hempfield " had foregathered there according to plan. It was already tiring of waiting Daunt's return from his reconnaissance when Ranger Simon Scull appeared. He told them that, at the first word of the project, he —fearing for Daunt's safety and desirous, moreover, of securing data at first hand—had himself crossed the Susquehanna and sought that suspected log-cabin on the deserted Joppa Trail.

My mouth went dry as I launched a final query:

" And what—whom," I stammered, " did they find? "

The ferrymen were little fellows with copper skin and noses like an eagle's beak. One was young; the other's straight hair had gone gray. It was the elder that now answered me:

" No man alive," said he. " They find only Knowles Daunt: him all dead."

And now the Law was scouring the west bank with a warrant for the arrest of Thomas Cresap on a charge of murder—and the Ranger of the Manor rode head-to-head beside the Crown Magistrate!

CHAPTER XXIII

THE KING OVER-THE-WATER

NOT long did I tarry with those ferrymen. They had loaves of bread and slices of smoked meat that made my hungry stomach yearn, yet a plea for food would be a hail to suspicion. Evidently, the affair of Knowles Daunt had overshadowed any word of my disappearance—perhaps even postponed Uncle Simon's mention of it—but if I lingered by the waterside, some question of my identity would inevitably arise; besides, time must be passing. So, loath as I was to leave the sight of refreshment, it was best soon to strike off up the York Highroad like a lad headed for home.

After a quarter-mile of travel, I circled and doubled through the woods to a sight of the ferry and there watched to see whether the posse returned within the time that remained to me. Then, as nothing of that sort occurred, and as the sun drew to my hour, I made my way back to the Anderson Trail and the forked road.

Hardly had I reached the trysting-place when I was informed that someone expected me. Out of the forest on the opposite side of the path from the lonely tree came a low whistle. I turned toward it and presently reached a little rill, and on a rock beside that sat, wrapped in his cloak, the Stranger.

"So," said he, "you made quick use of my message. I am glad to be of service."

His plumed hat was pushed back on his head, leaving his dark, handsome face all clear. He held out a welcoming hand.

"Then you weren't hit?" I cried.

"When they shot from the bank?" he countered. "Lad, I shall live to die on a scaffold in London Tower!" He drew me to a seat on the rock beside him. "Now, tell me what can be done, meantime, for you."

It was necessary then to put a hard question, but I put it boldly:

"Sir, are you Thomas Cresap?"

He threw back his head and laughed. It made a fine showing of his white teeth.

"You may trust to my discretion," said I, blushing; but I stuck to my guns.

"I warrant I may! But why," he demanded, "do you ask?"

"Because," I put it flat, "I won't serve a man that does what he does in the way he does it."

It was plain that he liked my bluntness. He clapped me on the shoulder. "Serve?" he echoed, and then said: "Well, on my word as a gentleman, though I be much else perhaps, Cresap I am not. Now out with the rest of it."

The relief was great. Though I could not see how he could be a cut-throat, yet I had feared in spite of reason.

" In that case," I vowed, " if you are highwayman or no, I'll stay with you."

" So," says he, yet showing no surprise, only a certain puzzlement, " is not this decision something of the suddenest? I thought your honor bound you across the river. I'll have none with me whom honor ought to range on the other side."

" And I," I cried, " know no code of honor that binds me to a murderer!" And forthwith, touching first upon my indenturing, I told him how my uncle had sent word to Lancaster that the Stranger was Cresap, and what, this morning, I had seen in the clearing beside the Joppa Trail.

He heard me with a corrugated brow, his dark face serious beyond the common. His chin pressed into his closed fist, his elbows were propped upon his knees.

" Why don't you denounce this assassin?"

" Because I am now a runaway servant, and he is the Ranger of the Manor. Who would take my word against his? Oh," I broke off, " why did he do this thing? Why did he do it?"

" He did it," said the Stranger, " to make matters worse for me."

THE RANGER OF THE SUSQUEHANNOCK

My friend explained his view of the killing. Uncle Simon was of course in some treacherous communication with Cresap and the Marylanders. There were perhaps evidences at the log-cabin which, when he learnt of the proposed attack on it, he went forward to destroy, but certainly he had another purpose.

" The Ranger," said the Stranger, " has denounced me as Cresap. I gather he is not liked by his neighbors; I misdoubt if he is overly cherished by his superiors in the government; only that evil Susquehannock loves him, who fears him, too, and loves no other creature. Yet the rulers of new countries may not be too particular of their lieutenants: Harley has found that Simon Scull works with such good purpose in his department as to stifle inquiry of his method. Lacking convincing proof, his accusation of an unknown—and I am none to bear great investigation!—must have final weight. Now he heads an incensed posse against me as a recent murderer of one of their own fellows."

The Stranger plucked at a near-by bush. He hesitated, but then, with a shrug, continued:

" The words with which I gained entrance to ' Lynton ' roused in Scull, no matter why, a fear that makes him want to shut my mouth forever. Well, here is his opportunity. That posse finds me; righteous wrath in the man overcomes proper caution in the officer: he shoots me down—and there am I out of his way, and he, moreover the freer to deal with Cresap, since Cresap will, at least for a time, be thought to have died in my person."

It was a devilish scheme, but plain enough now, and it made me all the more eager to remain with my friend. As to that, the Stranger presented difficulties: the life would be hard, each hour crowded with danger; he could not find it in his conscience ——

But I interrupted him: "If I go not with you, where can I go?"

He nodded. "And I should tell you, too, that I am no highwayman, either. Only, lad—lad—how can I risk you in a cause that is not yours?"

"But," I said, "it *is* mine!"

"How so?" He looked at me sharply. "What do you know of it?"

"Nothing," said I, "and yet more than enough. Any cause of yours must be mine, for you came to 'Lynton' in my father's name."

At that the Stranger sprang to his feet. He caught my face in both his hands and studied it as if it had been a portrait.

"Egad," says he, "the same straight hair—Frank would never curl his—the same brown eyes—aye, and the same sallowness, too, that's somehow not a blemish! I should have guessed it: only for your speaking of Scull as an uncle, I should have done so. This man you call 'Uncle' is your *step*-uncle—and you are Frank Rowntree's own son!"

He sprang back and performed one of those French hat-flourishes that he so loved.

"I was too long exiled across the Channel," he then said, "ever to have seen you in England, but I have heard of you from Frank. Greatly my senior as he was, your father was the best of my friends. Why, once in an Italian brawl, he saved my life, and I have dedicated this year to that debt's repayment. Master Nicholas Rowntree, I am Sir Geoffrey Faulkner, like yourself a runaway, but like yourself a runaway only from injustice."

I had heard his name as that of one of the bravest and most irreconcilable supporters of the Stuart cause against those Hanoverians who had the British throne, and now he told me something of his own story and something more of mine. He told me, in fine, how I stood with Simon Scull.

"Oh," said he, "this excellent step-uncle of yours came into the Ravenscar estates honestly enough, so far as the letter of the law's concerned! That Brunswick Dutchman, whom he calls his king, had his courts declare them forfeit when your father was arrested, and then conferred them on yon Scull. He had not the temerity to confer the title along with them, but all the lands he gave. And what was the purchase-price, think you? These usurpers never give much for nothing. Thirty pieces of silver—the Field of Blood—the Potter's Field! Pimpled Simon got all Ravenscar for betraying Frank Rowntree when Frank was Scull's own guest!"

My shocked mind reverted to my eighth birthday and that night of my father's return. I remembered how Uncle Simon had left the castle, and how the Hanoverian soldiers entered it. Again I tiptoed barefoot down the stairs; again I saw the candle-light fall on the strange faces and the intruders' uniforms; again I watched my parents in their last embrace.

" Why did my mother never tell me this? " I asked.

" She never knew. How could she guess such treachery? We exiles ourselves learned it only lately from a captured spy." Sir Geoffrey took me by the hand. " But now you know who was the traitor, Nicky, and I know you—and there be more than a few wrongs that we should set right together."

I think it was then I made some boyish inquiry whether, if the Ranger were so falsely come by his wealth, the indenture tying me to him could be legal.

" Legal enough in the Hanoverian's courts, no doubt," laughed my friend, " but binding in honor— never. If you need not serve a murderer, need you serve a murderer-thief? Why, boy, the very money he paid to buy you would have been yours through inheritance but for his treason. So long as you are not caught, so long are you safe."

But all this talk of wealth put yet another idea into my head.

" Why, then," said I, " if the Ravenscar lands would have been mine, would the jewels have been mine also? "

" Jewels? " says Sir Geoffrey, and he leapt back half a yard. " What's this about jewels? "

The attic at " Lynton " and the box-within-a-box that was hid there: I informed him of it.

He fell atremble with excitement. Out of his dark eyes gleamed that light which comes to one who sees, near at last, the triumphant ending of a long quest.

" Confirmation! Why, Nick, this was that, sending Harley ahead, I came to the New World to determine and secure. Now will one clear your father's name in his own party. I knew Frank Rowntree could never have hypothecated them for his own uses; I killed one man in duel for saying so! "

These were all the ejaculations of a high excitement, but they stirred my head to yet another memory. It was the memory of my father's whispered words to my mother, that same night of his arrest:

" Tell Simon where I have hidden them, and bid him keep them safe for . . ."

But laughing Sir Geoffrey Faulkner had laid a slim hand on me and was shaking me in the grip of a lion.

" No," he was saying, " those jewels are not yours, Nicky; nor mine, nor yet your uncle's—no, nor your father's either. Ripped from their setting by James II, but left to the keeping of a friend in his flight, those are the Crown Jewels of Britain and still the property of the King—and you and I shall yet recover them!"

His grasp hurt me. I broke away, but I caught fire from the light in his eyes.

"The King?" I gasped. "Which King?"

Sir Geoffrey's hat was in his hand again, and between his lips issued a snatch of once familiar song. It was "The Lass O' Morven," that sad old Jacobite ditty which had once been my lullaby, but now its pathos swelled to the fanfare of victory:

> "Over the water to Jamie—over the water to Jamie!
> Stand, and we'll sing:
> 'Here's to the King'"——

He broke off and swept his hat in the direction of the river. It was a gesture that changed the Susquehanna into the English Channel.

"Which King?" says he. "Why, there is but one true King back there, and that's he who is over the water from our native land." He made so wide and deep a flourish that the black plumes first brushed my cheek and then swept the moss at his boot-toes. "Jamie's son and heir Jamie—the Chevalier de St. George—His Majesty James Francis Edward Stuart, still, by the Grace of God, rightful King of England, Scotland and Wales!"

CHAPTER XXIV

WHAT WAS IN THE BOX

S O it was that, close by the spring on Anderson's Trail, in the County of York and Province of Pennsylvania, I came to know the worst that had happened to my family's fortunes at Castle Wyke, in the North Riding of Yorkshire.

History has long since informed all the world how the late King James II, at the time of his flight from the unhappy field of Drogheda—which the victors called the Battle of the Boyne—was forced to go so swiftly first to Dublin and then to Cork (whence he escaped to France) that he was separated from many of his most loyal supporters; and the incautious letters of Lord Clarendon's daughter have informed gossip that among those left behind was one into whose keeping had been given the Crown Jewels of England as long before as the day when His Majesty threw the Great Seal into the Thames on his way to Sheerness. The name of that custodian Mistress Hyde's very folly hesitates to mention, and discretion silences me, since, even at this late day, the Whigs might yet attempt vicarious vengeance. Enough is it that the gentleman in question, being himself hotly pursued, passed his commission to another, and he to a third, and that so, at last, the trust fell upon my father, then little more than arrived at man's estate. That was the beginning of our ruin.

My father, the last Lord of Ravenscar, was not positively known to have fought for the Stuarts at Boyne Water. He returned to Wyke Castle, openly unmolested—under the terms of the Act of Pardon and Indemnity—but quietly watched—as well he knew—by the creatures of the so-called William III.

His every movement was observed, yet he intended to take the jewels abroad himself at the earliest opportunity, or else to commit them to transfer by one of those messengers who were continually crossing and recrossing the Channel between the rightful monarch and his supporters at home. This was not, however, to be. It was the fate of the exiled Stuarts to be surrounded abroad by almost as many traitors, spies and thieves in Whig pay as by their own friends. The usurpers were greedy for the jewels, and so command came to Lord Ravenscar to conceal his trust in his own home in England, where it would be least likely to be sought. Anne followed William and Mary on the throne, and the Hanoverian George succeeded Anne, and still this state of affairs went on.

Then came my father's first flight. Walpole's agents discovered him in a new-born plot for the restoration of the King-over-the-Water. The warning reached

Lord Ravenscar when he was from home, where the gems were hidden; he had to cross to France without them and this, as ill-luck would have it, at the very time when the James that was dead King James' son and heir decided he could now have them safely in his own keeping.

Some years passed, while I was a baby in Yorkshire and my father an exile abroad. At last slanderous tongues began to whisper that he had misappropriated the jewels to his own purposes. Lord Ravenscar, not knowing surely who was his friend—except the much younger Sir Geoffrey, then absent in the Low Countries—vowed that he would confute these traducers by his own act. He returned secretly to England to fetch the jewels, which he had left in a hiding-place at Wyke known to himself only. There it was he was arrested, having but time to whisper the secret of the gems' whereabouts to my mother and bid her inform Uncle Simon, who was to convey them to their proper owner.

So much I made out by piecing my own memories to what Sir Geoffrey Faulkner told me that evening, beside Anderson's Trail, and my informant said he had suspected what details I supplied. It was to retrieve the jewels, as well as my father's honor, that at his first, but delayed, opportunity he had stolen into England, made further inquiries and then, having dispatched Harley to prepare the way, followed Uncle Simon's path to Pennsylvania.

WHAT WAS IN THE BOX

"For," says he, as he clapped me again on the back, "'tis the Ranger of the Manor that betrayed Frank Rowntree's good name, as well as his liberty, and that stole the Crown Jewels of England!"

By the time this long tale had been told, the first shock of Scull's perfidy was somewhat lessened, yet I continued to wonder at his deed. I asked why, since my step-uncle's sympathies were not with the Stuarts, he had not given the gems to the usurping King George.

"Because," said Sir Geoffrey bitterly, "his sympathies are not even with the usurper, but with Simon Scull."

"Then why has he not sold the gems?"

"He dares not. He must attend for opportunities to dispose of them bit by bit, and opportunities of such sort are rare in a wilderness, though it was in a wilderness that he thought his person would be safest." Sir Geoffrey spat. "Phff, the vermin!" And then a new light shone from his eyes. "Egad, this is *our* opportunity, Nicky! Come, we shall fetch the jewels!"

His inspiration was clear. The posse was seeking him on this side of the river: "Lynton" was all but unguarded.

I was desperately hungry now, and very tired, but what were hunger and weariness in the light of this chance to redeem my father's honor? I tucked into my jacket the pistol that my companion gave me, and together we made a wide detour, through the woods and past a single and lonely large clearing therein, a turnip-field, and so at last reached a quiet spot beside the Susquehanna, where his boat lay concealed. Only one caution suggested itself.

"Are we not," I inquired, "to take your man Harley?"

"He is on Round Top, and there is no time to go for him," said Sir Geoffrey. "We must have been to 'Lynton' and away again before that posse abandon their search."

The sun, above the hills, painted half the river golden when we shoved off. Behind us rose the hooded peaks; before, lay the scattered plantations of the Lancaster County side and, well down-stream, on the York County shore, we could make out the ferry-boat, the ferrymen dozing on its deck, waiting the posse's return.

"There will be only a squaw at 'Lynton,'" said I: "a woman named Massáya; but she is a terrible creature and as strong as a tigress."

Sir Geoffrey laughed. "I never feared a woman yet, and it is the tigers among 'em that like me best."

Unobserved we crossed. We landed at the point from which Sir Geoffrey had put out in his escape from Simon and Constable Jones, for the pursuers must land at the ferry-stage, and that was a considerable distance off. Then I led Sir Geoffrey by the screen of bushes that had served me in my own departure. So we came to the corner of the barn, and I could again see Massáya, much as I had earlier seen her, through the open kitchen doorway. Her broad back was now toward us, but I whispered:

" She has eyes between her shoulders! "

" In that case," says Sir Geoffrey, " she much resembles the most of her sex, and we shall have to substitute speed for stealth. It suits me better. Are you ready? Now! "

He sprang into the clearing. Close at his flying heels I followed. In two dozen strides, he was half-way to the kitchen-door.

In six, Massáya met him. She had heard our onrush —which, indeed, we made no endeavor to muffle—and, instinctively understanding something of its nature, launched a sally from her fortress. There must have been firearms in that kitchen, but here again there assuredly was no moment to seize one: the squaw had been poking the fire, and she came at us with a four-foot poker, a murderous iron-bar, whirling it high above the snaky hair of her ugly head as lightly as if it were a willow-switch.

Sir Geoffrey wasted nothing on courtesy. The pair came together with a mighty smash, so that his head was butting her in the midriff before her deadly blow could descend. One of his arms shot up and seized her raised wrist. At the same instant, I dived headlong for her ankles and grabbed them. The combined assault sent us all three in a struggling tangle to the grass.

Massáya set up a gigantic roar for help.

" Stop that! " cried Sir Geoffrey, and, rising to his knees, stuck a pistol against her head. " Nicky," said he: " rope! "

I ran to the stable and got some. When I came back, he had crammed the better part of her apron into that wide mouth.

Swiftly, and with the fingers of experience, he trussed her up. She made a load that exceeded our powers of convenient carrying, and so we dragged her, gagged and bound, into the house. We laid her on the miserable bed in what had been my own room and shut the door of it upon her malignant gaze.

" And now," said Sir Geoffrey, smacking his hands together as if to knock dirt from them—" now for the jewels."

Up the stairs we ran, which I had climbed so carefully through that last autumnal thunder-storm, and came to the landing whence my step-uncle and I had rolled in angry embrace. There the door was locked, but a few kicks from Sir Geoffrey's booted foot, a straining with his shoulder, and the wood crashed wide: we entered on the loose boards of the attic.

" There it is! There is the chest! " I said, and pointed to it.

His clasp-knife forced it. I swung back the lid. His fingers swept aside the mass of covering papers; he drew out the smaller box and plied his blade against it.

WHAT WAS IN THE BOX

The pale light of the early-winter sun filtered through the mullioned window, and a single ray, in which the moats danced merrily, was directed full upon the chest and the tall figure of Sir Geoffrey as, the box in his hand, he knelt on the littered boards. With itching fingers and bated breath, I bent over that sturdy shoulder.

The lock was strong, the case tough. There came a sharp splintering of steel, and his knife snapped; blade and hilt flew wide and clattered to the floor.

Our time might well be brief. "Make haste!" I gasped, and the sweat stood out on my own hands as if it were they that did this labor.

The man rose. Anger knotted his dark brows. He stepped toward the unplastered wall beside the window. Raising the box high overhead, he beat it against the rough, unplastered stones. Again and again he beat it against them. The shattering blows filled the attic with their clamor.

There was a rending of wood. The lid flew wide, but nothing dropped from the upturned receptacle.

The box was empty.

Only then did I remember what I had seen when Simon Scull fell from his mare on the Wilderness Road near Philadelphia, and the puffiness of his jacket this very morning.

"He carries the gems with him whenever he is from home," said I, and, with many self-accusations for my stupidity, began to tell Sir Geoffrey the signs I should not have forgotten.

He cut me short:

" No matter now, Nicky. Had you remembered, I had not thought a man could forever be dragging a king's ransom about with him. You had seen this treasure: mayhap Scull has thought best to shift its hiding-place. I doubt that, for his position here secures him against you; yet, be it as it may, we can but await a better opportunity."

I had no heart for postponement. " Can we not stop here and seize the Ranger on his return? "

" He will not come alone."

" But you," I protested, " first arrived here quite un-aided to beard him."

Sir Geoffrey was no man to brook argument. " Pah! " said he. " Then I thought to browbeat him; now I know that he would denounce me as Cresap and have me hanged before I found any to believe my ac-cusations of him. If I am to command, I must be obeyed. Follow! "

He ran down-stairs, and I after him. We left our prisoner where we had stowed her, and hurried to the boat. Once on the river, Sir Geoffrey softened. He faced me with a slight smile.

" I have a cave at Round Top," said he, " that the faithful Harley has made almost fit for gentlemen. There we must wait our next chance. No man can find that cave, and, found, it is the sort of position that it is a joy to defend."

But I was not to see the cave on Round Top that afternoon, nor for many a day to come.

CHAPTER XXV

THE RIOT ACT

WE were engaged in drawing up our boat to its hiding-place on the York County shore when we caught sight of the posse reboarding their ferry-boat.

" So they have given us up," said Sir Geoffrey.

" We were none too soon," said I.

Soon enough we were, however, for our purpose. It was to see an act that I have never forgotten and that will have its place in another book, one day, when the history of Pennsylvania is written. It has all to do with the turnip-field whereof I spoke as lying between our landing-place and Anderson's Trail, and the cause was Magistrate Wright's determination to get in his turnips, now that he found himself so near them. Accompanied by two Shawanese servants, he had left the posse and come to where we speedily observed him.

A cart-road for farm-wagons passed hither through the forest, connecting, as I now know, with one of Mr. Wright's several west-shore farms: one which fronted the York Highway at a point beyond where I had turned northward in the morning. This field was a far outlying portion of that farm. It lay on slightly rising

198

ground, and at its end stood a log-house, once a dwelling, but, since the beginning of the Cresap raids, deserted. Circling the field, Sir Geoffrey and I now came to the knolltop behind the house and could look out over both house and field and, what none could do on the lower level, see some distance down the cart-road.

In the field were Mr. Wright and his pair of workingmen, about to begin their task. Up the road, as yet concealed from them, rode an armed party.

I thought at first this was the posse come back, and urged haste. My companion shook his head.

"There is the posse"—and he pointed—"on the river and half-way across. I wager these be Marylanders just arrived, and they mean no good to yonder Magistrate."

He was right. They came riding into the field now, and I counted thirty of them bearing blunderbusses and flourishing pistols and rifles, and one of them, a ferret-looking fellow in a bright green cap, pounding on a drum. Mr. Wright's servants ran for the house; the Magistrate, his narrow face thrust forward and his pigtail sticking straight out behind, stood still and gazed at the invaders.

"Are they soldiers?" I asked.

"Not they," Sir Geoffrey answered. "Belike they dishonor that name by calling themselves so, but I can tell that they are more dangerous than soldiers: they are a mob, Nicky."

He began to tiptoe down among the trees, and I with him.

When we had reached the wood's edge, and were crouched there, looking cautiously out, the mob had halted. It had halted because of the quick action and violent eyes of the Quaker. He was walking slowly up to the drum-beater at the head of the column.

" Stand back! " cried that one.

" Come on at your peril! " yelled another and levelled his flint-lock.

I caught at Sir Geoffrey's cloak. " We must save him," said I.

" Wait," said Sir Geoffrey.

Mr. Wright seemed not to hear the threats that were hurled at him. He advanced some paces more until his outstretched hand fell on the bridle of the horse bestrode by the ferret-faced drummer. His words came short and sharp.

" What is the meaning of this display? "

I thought surely they would shoot him then. Instead, some of the threatening weapons were lowered.

" What right," stormed the ferret-faced green-cap, " have you to ask? This is Maryland ground, and we be Marylanders come to seize it! " He swore vilely, but the hand that thrust the drumstick in his belt did not feel for his pistol.

" As for whose land it is," said Mr. Wright, " let the law decide ——"

" We'll none of the law-courts! " shouted somebody.

" Nay, we've had enough o' 'em! " called another.

And a third bellowed: " Shoot him down and burn the house, lads! "

The noise of their own voices encouraged them. They pressed their horses around the Quaker, but he evenly continued:

" And as for my right to ask your purpose, I am Crown-Magistrate in these parts, and you are a riotous assemblage gathered against the peace of this Commonwealth and of His Majesty."

Hoots answered him and jeers. One fellow struck off his wide-brimmed hat and another thrust a pistol under his nose.

I made sure he was no better than dead. I half rose. " We *must* help! " I whispered.

But again Sir Geoffrey commanded " Wait "—and pulled me down.

Mr. Wright drew a little book from his pocket and began to read. It was one of the bravest deeds that ever I have seen, for there were those thirty ruffians crowding 'round to kill him, and there he read them, unhurriedly and in level tones, the Riot Act and, at its conclusion, commanded them to disperse in the name, as he said, of " King George—God bless him! "

Some of them were moved, if not by the law, at least by this courage of its lone officer. They looked at him in a wonder that was half admiration.

" Sh!" chuckled my companion, " I could have wagered I had not misjudged him!"

Ferret-face, however, turned his back on Mr. Wright and, gesticulating and swearing wildly, bade the gang come on and make the man their prisoner. A few roared with him; two or three tittered, and somebody in the thick of the press cried out:

" Why don't you do it yourself, Jock? You're the closest!"

The laugh that followed this gave Mr. Wright another chance to speak. He raised an empty hand.

" So much for one law," he said, " and though you see I am unarmed "—for the only guns in his party his pair of servants had run away with into the house—" yet will I die defending it. And now for another and even greater Law."

" Great Hercules," whispered Sir Geoffrey at my elbow, " this is the strangest Magistrate I have ever met with: I vow he means to preach to 'em!"

And preach he did.

Many's the sermon I have heard since, and some not very poor. General Washington likes them dry and, for choice, from a Church of England minister; my two boys preferred them of the sharp, scolding sort that good Father O'Connell used to give us when we went to Snaketown—which is now Harrisburg; but never one more moving have I heard than that which this queer

Quaker launched in the turnip-field, like infallible bullets, at his outnumbering enemies.

I recall that he made his text " This is the Law which Moses set before Israel," and that he developed how God's law ordained the laws of men and obedience to them; that he proved that it took more courage to obey than to revolt. How he would have conformed this doctrine to his subsequent espousal of the Colonies' cause against the crown I know not, for I am no theologian; but that afternoon, he spoke with such a passion of sincerity as to remind me of St. Paul preaching to those who would slay him; and even as the Apostle to the Gentiles succeeded, so did he.

At first, they all interrupted; then only Ferret-face. Next, at a pause, even as with St. Paul, " some cried one thing, some another." And finally, with a burst of eloquence on the obligations of citizens, this Preacher-Magistrate came to a full end and only the planter remained.

" So there you are," says he, " a gang of you; and here am I a planter anxious but to get his turnips in. I have told you where your duty lies: if still you think it brave to rob me and burn my house, attempt it—and be hanged to you! "

Whichever won the most, the sermon or the courage of its preacher, won they were. Ferret-face danced before them, shrieking imprecations; but they protested that this Quaker was a brave fellow after all, and that they would not harm him; and with that, when someone shouted that they would help with his crop, why spades were brought from the house, and, ere we well understood it, that whole crowd of intending murderers were assisting Mr. Wright's servants dig up the turnips and pile them in the cabin.

Under cover of the woods, Sir Geoffrey fell a-laughing.

" Who says," he asked, " the days of miracles are over? "

We watched the work, and saw disgruntled Ferret-face ride away down the cart-track. One turnip rolled to the forest's edge, and I made a dart for it. Sir Geoffrey hauled me smartly back.

" Are you mad? " says he.

" I am hungry," I said, and told him that I had eaten naught since an early and scanty breakfast.

He called himself a bad commander and led me, out of temptation's way, to the knolltop, where he produced from his cloak a half-loaf of bread and a flask of water. You may wager that I made a clean meal of it.

While I ate, the work below ended, and the Marylanders—each man sheepishly shaking Mr. Wright by the hand and receiving his thanks and some silver, too, so long as the money in his purse lasted—mounted and filed away. Sir Geoffrey, who was never hungry while action was afoot, watched them go. Presently, he climbed a tree and looked toward the York Highroad.

"Nicky," said he, "that is the last of those fellows, but not the last of this invasion. They wisely left a rear-guard behind them when they came here: I had not credited them with so much military wisdom. Well, did you mark that green-capped drummer? The main body he cannot persuade to return, but he's won that rear-guard, who had not the benefit of Wright's eloquence—and, egad, he is bringing them back with him!"

I stood up. "How many?"

"Fifteen, with the leader." He loosed his sword in its scabbard. "And I doubt if that leader will risk any parley this time: he'll charge. Come, lad: we shall be needed now!"

Already he was striding down the knoll. Before, I had wanted to help the planter; now I remembered that we were fugitives from justice and should be delivering ourselves to a Magistrate. But Sir Geoffrey shook his dark head.

"Nay, Nicky," said he, "I owe this Quaker a good turn for his rescue of me from Scull's red Indian—and oh, but I like his courage, too! Our disappointment at good Simon's house has disturbed my temper. I'm sick for a fair fight: that's the truth of it—and I never saw a gentleman better worth fighting for than this same preacher!"

Me he offered to send back, but I would none of that. We came together to the house and walked in at the door, where Mr. Wright and his two Shawanese servants stood among their gathered turnips.

The Magistrate showed none of the surprise that he must have felt, but his brown eyes sparkled.

" So," he said, " it's thee, eh? And this runaway-boy in thy perverting company. Are all the rogues in America gathering at this spot to-day? "

Sir Geoffrey only executed a flourishing salute. Briefly he stated the danger and proffered our help.

Mr. Wright heard him unruffled:

" Then thee's not Cresap? "

" Not even partly, sir."

" Ah, well, I thought that might be one of Friend Simon's mistakes. But thee's the fellow that met me on the Wilderness Road, or I am much mistaken."

" Whom you saved there, sir," said Sir Geoffrey— " and therefore at your service."

I knew that Mr. Wright, gazing at us so intently, was debating whether this were not Cresap after all and the whole thing a trap. He seemed to decide in the negative, for, says he presently:

" I shall gratefully accept thy help, as a man; but, as a Magistrate, I must not forget thy offense. Thy deeds this afternoon may mitigate sentence, but thee is to remember that a crime is a crime. Should we drive off these ruffians, even by thy aid, I shall deem thee my prisoner."

Neither to the scrutiny of himself nor to this warn-

ing had Sir Geoffrey appeared to vouchsafe any attention: he had struggled back through the turnips to the
doorway and been peering out.   Now, without at once
turning, he made answer:

"My trial and sentence may befall in a higher court
than yours, Master Magistrate, and in another world.
For, though not yet visible, there comes the second set of
Marylanders, and they outnumber us three to one."

CHAPTER XXVI

THE BATTLE AT THE HUT

"HOUSE" was scarce the word for that building we five were now called to defend against fifteen. It was perhaps twenty feet across and not much more than twelve deep, nor was there a second story. As it backed on the knoll, there was no window at that end, but only a fireplace. Windows were one on each side of the hut, and two were at the front, with the door between them.

"A word more," said Mr. Wright, "in explanation. Reading out the law of the King to our enemy, I have done my duty as a Crown-Officer; preaching against riot as the Spirit moved me, I have justified my position as a member of the Society of Friends; but now "—and here a certain satisfaction pushed into his voice—" now that they attack despite all I may do—why, I have the right to defend my property, and that right I propose to exercise."

Sir Geoffrey smiled. The speaker saw it and, in glancing away, saw also that all the hut's floor was covered by those turnips dug out of the sloping field before us.

THE BATTLE AT THE HUT

"Clear these from the firing-stations," Mr. Wright commanded. "We must have no poor footholds."

He spoke with the quiet authority of a veteran officer, and I looked at him in amazement. His deep-set eyes had the glint of steel in them; he was bareheaded, and his pigtail still stuck out like an Admiral's. In his encounter with that first set of ruffians and the zeal of his sermon, his dress had been so disturbed as to lose something of its repose: altogether he looked little the Quaker.

"Come, come!" said he, and his order was executed.

There was not time to bare all the floor, but the turnips lying beside windows and at the doorway were hastily tossed upon the hearth. Even Sir Geoffrey helped in that task.

"My faith, Mr. Wright," said he, "when the law made you a magistrate, the army lost a good soldier!"

Mr. Wright's freckled face blushed a little.

"I am no believer in violence," he answered; "but if I am to be attacked in my own house, why I shall make the best resistance possible."

"Well spoken!" Rising, Sir Geoffrey threw a final turnip into the fireplace. "How many guns have we?"

"There are three with us."

"And my pistols. I shall want the pair. Nicky, hand me that which I lent you."

I pretended not to hear.

"We shall be so outnumbered," said the Magistrate,

" that much will depend upon careful marksmanship. Thomas," he told one of the Shawanese, a tall fellow with a single feather in his hair, " do thee defend that window on the left side.—David "—this was for the other Indian, a little man with a keen eye—" draw and bolt the shutters on the right; then half-close the door and fire, when the time comes, around it. I shall take this front casement. Thee, friend," and he now addressed Sir Geoffrey, " will be at the corresponding one."

The Shawanese did as bid. Mr. Wright had accounted for all the obvious fighting-stations. In the farthest corner, I made myself quietly busy with the turnips, for I feared that he might hide me somewhere, and that I was determined should not be. It was quite vain. The Magistrate went to a table in the middle of the room (it was the sole piece of furniture remaining) and on it piled the shot and powder horns.

" Boy, can thee load a gun? "

Sulkily, I told him yes, I could.

" No man that has fired will leave his station. This lad will reload for us all."

" So give me my pistol, Nicholas," grinned Sir Geoffrey.

" But I want to fight! " I protested.

" Thee will load," said Mr. Wright.

" Sir ——" I began.

The Magistrate merely pointed to the table. I met

his eyes only an instant; then, tossing Sir Geoffrey's pistol petulantly to the floor, went where Mr. Wright ordered.

" Any sign of them? " that one demanded.

The Indian David was peeping 'round the door. " No see, but hear."

" All the arms are loaded? "

Each defender replied in the affirmative.

So we waited, every potential fighter at his post and one disgruntled powder-monkey in the centre.

It seemed to me that we waited very long. I leaned toward the door.

" Keep your place! " said Mr. Wright, without turning, and I jumped back to it.

The silence was heavy. At last our commander spoke again:

" No one will fire until the Marylanders shall have done so. Then pick your man with care."

It was Sir Geoffrey's turn to protest:

" Yet, sir, they are sure not to fire until they have reached the house, and then they will be upon us, and we overcome by numbers."

" Thee has the bearing of a military-man," said Mr. Wright: " be so good as to assume the obedience also."

I laughed aloud, but my laughter was cut short by a cry from David in the doorway:

" They come now! "

It was so much what all had been anxiously awaiting

that I was forgotten, and my curiosity could indulge itself undeterred. I peeped over David's head.

Out of the cart-track's mouth and spreading into a front at the base of the hill, came the fourteen new Marylanders, all afoot now, and behind them the bright green cap of the man with the ferret's face. One fellow carried a blunderbuss; the rest were armed with rifles.

In my excitement, I bent forward too far. That Shawanese was crouched with his weapon at his shoulder, his finger on the trigger. I touched him; he was startled, and he fired.

" Thank God! " cried Sir Geoffrey.

I leapt back to the table.

" David," said Mr. Wright, " I shall deal with thy breach of discipline later. And as for thee, Friend "— to Sir Geoffrey—" think shame to thyself for thanking thy Maker for a disobedience! "

The smoke had cleared away. Even from my position, I could see that the man with the blunderbuss was fallen and that the line wavered. I heard a voice I recognized as Ferret-face's shouting:

" Come on, lads! There are but three of them! "

At that cheerful reminder, the line must have begun to advance, and a rattle of shots sounded, bullets beating against the logs of the house like hail. It was the first time I had heard lead spatter around me in anger, but I was too wrought upon by the joy of battle to regard it. David's disobedience had drawn the enemy's fire; our side was free to answer; the hut became a cavern of explosions.

Thereat we all joined together in spirit. Sir Geoffrey, declaring that his pistols would not yet carry and that there was no danger from Thomas's side, seized that Shawanese's weapon and shot from his own window.

"There goes another!" said he, and tossed the arm to me for reloading.

Mr. Wright's gun barked. "I fear I have killed one poor fellow!" he shouted, and the exultation of his tone belied the words' meaning.

The hut was full of smoke, and I was, in any event, kept too busy with ramrod and powder to see aught, but I heard another hostile volley.

"Hurry!" cried the fighting Quaker. His extended fingers worked in eagerness for the gun with which I was engaged.

"Missed!" I heard Sir Geoffrey call at a failure of his own, and the feathered Thomas, with one of my friend's relinquished pistols, was firing futilely over David's head.

Nevertheless, I understood that our more circumspect marksmanship was telling, and I felt strangely at ease. Sweating over my task, I had no chance to regret the loss of a better one, and yet a strange return of my hunger came upon me, and I stopped for half a second to stoop and raise a small turnip to my ready mouth. At that moment:

" Here they are! " Sir Geoffrey vociferated. " Club your guns! "

He poked his own into a face that filled his appointed window, and then we all sprang toward the doorway as the attackers crowded in.

Not two of us reached it. The enemy piled over David, into whom, in the mêlée, I plainly saw the ferret-faced man, though he was well at their rear, stick a knife. But neither they nor we went far. The loose turnips in the room's centre wrought a common destruction. Reloading and returning weapons, I had been able to go among them safely; but in this stampede there was no picking of one's way. The hard spheres rolled impartially under the feet of defenders and attackers alike, and both parties tumbled, in a sputter of pistol-shots and curses, to the floor.

It was too much for the Marylanders. They thought some new and terrible form of resistance had been de-vised for their reception, and to this was added the real-ization that the Pennsylvanians had been reënforced by Sir Geoffrey and myself. Upon the skulls of some of them a few blows descended, but soon the survivors, now reduced to a trio, with the green-capped ferret in the lead, had revolved to the doorway and there risen. An instant later, they were running down the hill.

" Enough! " ordered Mr. Wright. He had suddenly remembered something of his Quaker principles. " They are beaten—let them go! "

But Sir Geoffrey was now past all restraint. Drawing his sword, he plunged after the runaways, and I circled the Magistrate and followed.

Sir Geoffrey outdistanced me, and two of the Marylanders outdistanced him. Half-way down the field, however, the third fellow tripped. I saw him start to get up: it was Ferret-face.

The name was deserved. His nose seemed to grow sharper; his long teeth showed, and against the approaching Sir Geoffrey, who bore only his sword, the green-capped rogue raised a cocked pistol.

My friend scorned to pause or even deviate. He was a fair mark.

I had come out too quickly to seize a weapon. What was to be done?

Ferret-face took careful aim.

I started to cry out and found my mouth stopped. The attackers had rushed into the hut as I bit that turnip. Their advent must have found other uses for my hands: there had been the turnip through all that followed, and there was it still with my teeth sunk into it, half-way in my mouth.

A stone might have served as well, but I thought not of that. I jerked out the turnip and threw it with all a lad's might and all a schoolboy's practised skill.

Ferret-face saw me, and saw it coming. But too late. It took him between the eyes. His pistol exploded harmlessly. He turned and ran. Ere Sir Geoffrey had discovered the source of his rescue and cried his thanks, it was bootless to follow; but at least my friend was safe.

CHAPTER XXVII

DANGEROUS WORK

SIR GEOFFREY turned up the field toward the hut, at the door of which Mr. Wright was standing.

"No, no!" I cried, catching my companion's hand. "Don't go back there!"

"And why not?" says he.

"Have you forgot," I asked, "that he said you would still be his prisoner? We have the start: let us run for it!"

Sir Geoffrey shrugged. "Why, as to that, I can't. Since I remained to fight for this Magistrate after he had stated his conditions, I gave him, in a manner of speaking, my parole.—Of course *you* are free to go, Nicky."

That concluded my appeal. "I go where you go," said I; and together we ascended to the hut.

Mr. Wright's greeting evinced no approval of our honorable return. "I ordered no pursuit," said he, "and you two disobeyed me."

Sir Geoffrey swept his plumes to both of us. "Thanks to this boy's turnip, no harm happened; but

217

I have the honor to report, commander, that the enemy are in full retreat."

" Thee thinks they will not come back? " inquired the Magistrate, smiling in spite of himself.

" Not they, sir."

" The ferry-boat is to return for me. Does thee think they will not try to waylay us at the landing? "

" I think that they won't stop running until they have reached their horses, and that they will gallop until they pass the true Maryland border."

" Come inside," said Mr. Wright.

The smoke had cleared from the hut's interior, revealing an ugly picture. Just beyond the door lay the Shawanese David, lately so zealous a defender, weltering in a pool of blood and quite dead. Beyond him, at the table, his fellow-Indian, Thomas, tore his shirt into strips to staunch a flowing wound in his shoulder. Among the trampled and reddened turnips, writhed two of the enemy, who groaned from badly battered heads, and one that would never utter sound again. It was my first sight of a battle's aftermath and turned me a little sick.

" Their other dead," said Sir Geoffrey, " they have left in your turnip-field, Master Magistrate."

Mr. Wright's keen eyes considered him from their caverns. " So that I have four only captives, Mr. Prisoner? "

" Including me and Nicky, sir? " My friend

218

shrugged. "Well, by your leave, a quiet word on this subject that we were discussing when the little dance began. I have terms of surrender to offer."

I think that Mr. Wright would have refused parley. He did mutter something about the nonsense of terms from a man already technically in custody, but Sir Geoffrey only laughed and tucked an arm under one of the Magistrate's, and led him back through the door, whither, after some private talk, he summoned me.

There my companion explained Mr. Wright's position in regard to the border-warfare. This recent skirmish (so he called it) was but one of many, and in itself counted for nothing. It was won, yet the situation as a whole remained desperate. Unless the Pennsylvanians could discover and put a stop to that organized treason which seemed constantly betraying their plans, the border-estates would soon be lost to Penn's Colonists and to all who held title under grant or purchase from the Penns: the Marylanders were slowly gaining ground; they must soon make forcible and permanent occupation.

I reflected that the price of some of those estates would have been my father's, but for my step-uncle.

"But you and I know ——" I began.

"Nothing for sure," Sir Geoffrey intervened, "and it is not yet time to tell the whole of what we suspect." He then addressed Mr. Wright again: "Sir, I do not count that I discharged my debt to you to-day, for what little I did here was no more than a relief to my over-burthened nerves: it was a personal indulgence. On your part, you, with good show of logic, consider me still amenable to your authority. Well, here I shall pay in full, and you will still be none the worse in your magisterial capacity, since I give you my formal parole —I, who could safely have broken a parole merely implied, had I chosen to run away when at the foot of this field, a few moments since; and I think," says he, " that I can give Nicky's, also? "

He looked at me with one of his humoring smiles. Without the least realization of what tended, I consented.

" 'Tis too great peril for a boy," objected Mr. Wright, who was none the less patently yielding to this suggestion made before I joined the pair.

" His record will be his safety, as will my record be mine. You have but to advertise our offenses, and we shall be welcomed whither we go. Besides, the presence of a boy confutes suspicion. Come, sir: you once did me the favor of saving my life; do I betray a lack of gratitude when I ask leave to surrender myself back to you a little time hence, laying this whole conspiracy by the heels? "

No man could win men like Sir Geoffrey! That preacher whose sermon had persuaded thirty ruffians was himself persuaded. With no more word to me than a friendly, but restrained, caution to guard myself, the

DANGEROUS WORK

Magistrate, assuring himself of his surviving servant's ability to make the journey, set off with Thomas to the ferry, directing merely that we watch the wounded Marylanders until we hear the approach of a party that he would send back so soon as he could collect it at dawn, to convoy them to Lancaster.

"When we get sound of that party approaching," said Sir Geoffrey, as we watched the pig-tailed Magistrate and Thomas move down the field, "we are to steal away. And now, Nicky, can you endure a supper of only raw turnips?"

I told him truly that I could eat anything, but that I wanted to know what was the further task to which he had pledged me.

"Lad, you pledged yourself," said he; "and, being no Simon Scull, well I thought that you understood its import. You are a resourceful boy and of right proper courage. What we are to do is, God willing, to serve as spies in Maryland."

The very mention of it called imperiously to my love for adventure. "But I had hoped," I said, "to be furthering, with you, my father's cause."

We were first bandaging and then binding the captives as we talked. "Your father's cause," he promised, "shall not suffer by our efforts, and I shall leave Harley to hide on Round Top and scout around 'Lynton.'"

Thus reassured, I was all eagerness for the expedition; but while we munched our scanty meal in the twilight before the hut, a seemingly insurmountable objection presented itself, and inwardly I called Nicholas Rowntree every sort of ingrate for his treatment of a faithful ally that he had for hours past forgotten.

"Oh, no," I mourned, "I cannot go with you!"

Sir Geoffrey fairly dropped a half-consumed turnip: "How's this?"

"I cannot go so far and leave the first friend that I made in America." And straightway I told him all about my faithful stallion, Success.

He chuckled a little, though not unkindly. "A worthy sentiment," said he, "and yet I turned a good horse loose in the woods ere paying my first visit at Simon's, while you—why, you left yours when you volunteered me your services."

"Ah, that," I explained, "put only a river betwixt us."

"Well, but what would you do? Stay with Harley? Go back to 'Lynton'? And as for first friends in America, have _I_ been an enemy?" He put me fairly on the horns of the dilemma, and then says he: "I dare not risk you across that river, but Harley shall fetch you your Success."

I brightened—and then remembered: "No man can touch Success but me, without I am there to direct him."

"You would not say so if you knew Harley: he was

born in a mews." Sir Geoffrey rose. " I have a plan. Give me your cap, lad." He snatched it from my head. " And now await me here."

He thrust a pistol into my hand and disappeared among the trees of the forest.

He was gone a long time. The night fell black, and colder weather with it. I thought of the dead so close beside me and of those other dead in the field below. As much as I could, I ministered to our wounded prisoners, stubbornly silent, and I believed that every woodland sound heralded the advent of some party for their rescue.

I tried to think of my father, so much worse off than me in his Tower-prison, but the smell of fresh blood tainted my nostrils, and with each movement of our captives I shivered. Mine was a chill and comfortless vigil, but at last Sir Geoffrey did reappear; he double-darkened the darkness of the doorway with the abruptness of a ghost.

" Ask me no questions; we must wait," said he.

And until close upon dawn we waited. He insisted that I wrap myself in his cloak, but I could not sleep in that charnel-house. I lay listening to Sir Geoffrey as he sat for hours humming " The Lass O' Morven " over and over again. I tossed about until the stars seen through the doorway began to pale, and a faint glow rose, far down the river, over the shoulder of that mountain we call Turkey Hill.

" They are here," said Sir Geoffrey.

Though I had heard nothing, I sprang up. " The men Mr. Wright told us he would send for the prisoners? "

Sir Geoffrey laughed. " *They* will have to wait the return of the ferrymen."

I could not understand why the ferrymen should make a crossing without the Magistrate's party, but I followed Sir Geoffrey's dim figure down the field, and, as I neared the cart-track, there came a whinny of recognition. I ran forward. Here came Harley, leading two horses, and one of them that poked his muzzle into my widespread arms was my own stallion.

" But how—how ——" I panted as I patted Success.

Harley made answer. He had stolen into Uncle Simon's stable; by his own horseman's arts and the pressure of my cap to Success's nose, he got safely away with his prize. The other horse was one that had been secured for Sir Geoffrey before the latter's arrival in America.

" And you crossed the river with mine? "

" No animal could swim it, Maester. The ferrymen were waiting the relief that the Magistrate's to send here. A pistol pointed at 'em paid my passage."

Still did I have my scruples. Even while embracing Success, I said to Sir Geoffrey: " Yet we must not steal my stallion."

" Was ever such a boy? " cried he. " Simon

224

Scull has naught in the world but is rightfully your father's!"

"Not by law," I protested. "No, Sir Geoffrey, you are tender of your balance with Mr. Wright; I must be tender of mine with Mr. Scull: I must pay for my horse."

There was a moment's silence; then: "Perhaps you are right," he admitted, "though it would not so have seemed to me."

"And I've no money," I lamented.

"Money!" That he said scornfully, and dipped his hand in his coat. "I'll lend it you—whatever sum you say. Only, though this horse must be excellent, yet, in these parts, he would not bring ten pounds."

"Not five 'e vouldn't, zur," supplemented Harley.

"I shall lend you five," said Sir Geoffrey, "and over-pay a rogue. Hurry, now. Harley will take it there another night and leave it where your precious uncle "—he referred to that relationship only when he wished to chide me—" where your uncle should find it. If his rascally servants steal it, that's no affair of ours."

"Lend me seven, please, sir."

He thrust the money into my hands. I gave it all to Harley.

"Can you write?" I asked.

"He can," said Sir Geoffrey. "And why, pray?"

"Because there are no writing-materials here for me," I said, "and I should like to send with this a letter, which he may pen to-morrow, telling Simon Scull that five pounds of this is for Success and two to free me of my debt to him."

CHAPTER XXVIII

IN THE ENEMY'S COUNTRY

ALMOST south we rode, Sir Geoffrey and I, until the sun was fairly at the zenith. The land was, of course, strange to us both, but our route was a bold following of the highway. Still in name a part of Pennsylvania, this district had been all but deserted by Pennsylvanians and was peopled—when there were any visible inhabitants—by Maryland squatters; the baser sort of Lord Baltimore's Colonists had pushed forward here. Should any questions be made of us, a part of the truth (the statement that we had separately fallen foul of the law in the north) ought to secure our welcome.

Harley we had left in our place at the hut. Sir Geoffrey feared that his servant's course with the ferrymen might send them back to "Hempfield" with a tale to change Magistrate Wright's grudging endorsement of our project:

"The Quaker is none too sure of me. His party that is to secure the prisoners might be sent over earlier and with instructions to pursue us. Once he has planned his retreat, a proper general never delays it: we'll be gone."

It was thus my general put the matter—but not until we had proceeded beyond any availing discussion of it!—and when I inquired of Harley's course:

" Why," said he, " Harley will do what Wright bade us do, and do it full as well. He will watch the prisoners until he hears the Hempfielders' approach, and then go safe to my cavern on Round Top. None can find him there, and thence, o' night, he will watch our interests for us."

I had wanted to see that hillside cave, and I remember asking why we did not visit it to outfit us for the journey.

" The less preparation our outfitting shows," my friend explained, " the more we shall seem fugitives to the Marylanders."

On such topics he discoursed freely enough, but upon the specific purport and details of our quest he rigorously maintained a military silence, nor do I now believe him to have had any real plan of action other than a trust in his own luck and daring. He had always found, he said, that Heaven favored a brave man facing odds in a just cause: it would not desert us once we had entered the lion's den.

" The sole way to detect a treachery," said he, " is at its source. Somehow down there "—and he pointed south—" we shall find the source of this one. Whom does your gallant uncle serve? Cresap, say you. And whom does Cresap serve? Why, Baltimore or his lieutenants. A confessed runaway, you cannot count on Wright's continued leniency if you remain near Hempfield; you cannot watch your Ranger there. By the same token, you cannot convict him by spying there on Cresap—nay, Cresap's self you have there no means of reaching. And so we ride, Nicky—whither we ride."

Once only I again insisted on what I had seen at the cabin along the Joppa Trail.

" For which," he sharply reminded me, " you have, as you said, but a fugitive-servant's word against that of a provincial officer. No more of this, so long as I command here! "

He was severe enough to still me for good and all. Then, a moment later, he had me surrender that one of his pistols which I had been carrying since our start and made me accept its mate instead, as the better of the brace.

The highway was fairly well constructed for so new a country, but, as I have said, it ran for the most part through a land deserted. Here and there we would come upon a neglected clearing and an abandoned cabin in its midst, mute tokens of the northward retreat of Penn's pioneers before the slow advance of the Marylanders; but gradually even these sad relics grew scarcer. There was only the thick woods around us, and we were glad enough to come upon an evil hovel where we could buy a little Indian-corn to roast for our midday dinner.

There were two men living here, villainous, low-browed fellows with shifting eyes, who quickly proved to be outposts of the enemy immigration. As was only natural in a new country, they showed a vast inquisitiveness about whence we came and whither we were going.

I was somewhat uneasy. Not so Sir Geoffrey.

" We are headed toward Annapolis," said he; and he proceeded jauntily with the half-truth upon which he relied: " As for the start of our travels, why, if you are honest supporters of the Calverts ———"

" Oh, aye, we're that! " they cried, and roared out an unclean jest.

" Why, then," my companion concluded, " there's no harm telling you that John Wright thinks us no better than we should be; and if a posse of his comes this way asking after us, you'll do us a kindness by forgetting we were here."

He had not to say more. I never imagined an adventurer who could be the gentleman and yet look, when he wanted, the highwayman so thoroughly as Sir Geoffrey. Those ruffians alcoholically grinned a sympathetic understanding that made me loathe the deception. They told us we need concern ourselves with no pursuit: no posse from Hempfield ever dared ride so far as this.

One day was greatly like another. The cold, as we went, became murderous, winter travelling from the north faster than we could make progress southward.

IN THE ENEMY'S COUNTRY

The wilderness was less and less broken, and though the valley which we traversed is one of the most lovely in the world, its rolling hills and gentle watercourses held little that could then inveigle my eye. Often a pack of deer would loiter across the road, and twice we saw brown bears in the thicket; the redmen had largely departed; the white were not yet fully come.

Better horses than ours proved there must seldom have been. Sir Geoffrey's mount—I called him " Corsair "—had excellent powers of both speed and endurance, and Success was as reliable for the heavy sort of work which at present we were engaged on as he had shown himself for racing in my dash from Lancaster to "Lynton." He responded to my very words; often he appeared to read my unspoken desires concerning him, and never once did he evince either fatigue or restlessness.

We now—from scattered settlers, desperate characters of this debatable tract—laid-in what rations-in-advance were possible, and sometimes had a fortunate shot at game, but as often as not we went hungry. So long as the sun shone we kept on our way; by night we turned into the forest for a troubled sleep. Sir Geoffrey ever made me share his wide cloak as a blanket; like all boys, I tossed and turned in my slumber, and more than once have I wakened to discover that he had surrendered to me the whole of our joint covering.

THE RANGER OF THE SUSQUEHANNOCK

Strictly as he avoided further talk of his immediate design, he was, however, loquacious enough on the deeds of his past, and never did lad have a better story-teller for companion. The last of his house, Sir Geoffrey, when scarce well in his 'teens, had been driven from England for loyalty to his family's Stuart-tradition, and from that day forward played the rôle of a soldier-of-fortune and champion of lost causes over half of Europe, always finding leisure to embroil himself deeper and deeper in the hundred-and-one plots for restoration of the old line to the throne of his native land.

He was with the Chevalier de St. George in the ill-starred attempt of 1708; he joined the Duc de Vendôme in time to meet defeat at Malplaquet. After the Peace of Utrecht and France's base renunciation of the Stuart cause, he fought for the Venitians against the Turks when the latter won Morea, left before the tide was turned and, though missing the start of the Scotch rebellion of '15, made junction with the Jacobites as they retired from Perth before the advance of Argyle. Not long later, he was back again for a part in that conspiracy of Charles XII of Sweden, when the papers of this monarch's ambassador were seized in London, and the records found of how the Spanish Minister Alberoni gave 1,000,000 livres toward a fresh invasion.

Sir Geoffrey sailed under Admiral Antonio de Castaneta to the catastrophe of Cape Passaro—shared the Stuarts' Spanish heyday—was one of the few men to reach Scotland's coast alive in the March of '19—escaped to the Continent—joined his hero in Italy, and acted as an emissary thence to Atterbury and to that perfidious politician and seductive philospher, Bolingbroke. In short, there seemed to have been no desperate venture during the last quarter-century but he had his part in it, and as he told these true tales with a vivid tongue and a fine gusto that scarce nodded to modesty, you may conceive that his conversation was my solace.

The longest journey has its end, however, and so had ours. It ended unexpectedly and with an incident that promised to upset Sir Geoffrey's plans, if he had any. Not many miles farther were we to ride southward in the light of day.

As gradually as it had been deserted, the country began again to give signs of human life. Cabins increased, and little farms, as we drew into that territory which was honestly the Marylanders', there grew more frequent signs of a proper tenantry's presence and fewer of the lees of pioneer humanity. So we too saw chance of faring better and, reaching one sunset, a small settlement, decided to put up at the inn around which it clustered.

We rode into a cobbled courtyard at its rear, and Sir Geoffrey called loudly for the tavern-keeper. A cross-eyed groom tried to take our horses, but Success would none of him, and it was plain I would have to feed and bed them myself, in the stable close under the inn-windows, while my companion fretted for the land-lord.

"He's a bit busy the night," the hostler apologized. "An unexpected party arrived only a few hours ahead of you."

Much confused talking from the tap-room confirmed this. However, the tavern-keeper appeared at last—a fat man, bald and rubicund.

"There is but one room left," said he.

"'Twill serve," Sir Geoffrey answered, but he spoke shortly, for I fancy he was used to commanding the best of any hostelry's attention.

"And it looks out on this stable-yard," the inn-keeper pursued. He pointed to a window on the floor above. "You see, sir, we are very full ——"

"Egad, then," cried Sir Geoffrey, "I won't eat with a crowd that shoves me over the mews. Take me there and have supper hurried up to us."

He passed indoors, ordering the meal, while I, having noted the assigned quarters, went about my task with the horses. So situate, ours could not be an inviting apartment, I reflected: events proved that it was most fortunate we got no other.

Some time later, when I had finished with the animals and patted Success good-night, I started to join Sir Geoffrey. Darkness had descended; the inn was ill lit; down-stairs it was crazily constructed, a rambling place, and I made one false turn: seeking the stairway, I blundered into the tap-room.

Perhaps a dozen men were there. They were booted and still marked as from a journey. Somehow, they seemed familiar. Then I stopped dead on the door-sill, for one of them was familiar indeed.

The light of a swinging lamp fell full on his face. Hatless it was—but it was the face of a ferret!

CHAPTER XXIX

"SPIES!"

I WHEELED. I stumbled down a passage and around a corner.

Had he seen me half so clearly as I saw him? Had he recognized me?

Providentially, I found the stairs, and our room at the head of them. Sir Geoffrey was seated at a table that groaned under its store of food. There was a place prepared for me; the waiter had withdrawn.

"Those men down-stairs!" I gasped. "They're the party that Mr. Wright turned back from the turnip-field ——"

"Close the door," Sir Geoffrey admonished me.

It was a proper precaution. I observed it and went on:

"The men Mr. Wright turned back; but it will be a different story now: he's not here—we are in their country—they will know us as spies—and that green-capped fellow I hit with the turnip, he's among them!"

Sir Geoffrey rose slowly.

"Did he see you?"

"I don't know."—My lips were dry, and my tongue too dry to moisten them. "I was quite clear at the tap-room door."

My commander took up his cape. " I am loath to lose this meal," said he; " it promised well for so poor a place." He bestowed a gravied roast in one of his cloak's capacious pockets. " Do not risk the interior of the house again, Nicky. Lower yourself from this window: windows seem better ways of exit than doors in this new country. Saddle the horses quickly, but quietly. I shall join you so soon as I have got my small belongings together and made sure of affairs here. Then we must ride again, my lad! "

I straddled the sill and swung from it. As if carried upon my shoulders, the cold dusk was descending on the enclosure, but I knew that there was not far to drop. So soon as my feet struck the cobbles, the window closed overhead, shut by Sir Geoffrey to veil the manner of my flight in case I had been recognized and should be too quickly traced to the room.

There came a continuous growl from the direction of the bar. It was a man's voice telling some tale that he did not relish, but its words were lost, and there was now no moment to spare for eavesdropping.

It was supper-time, and the courtyard was in consequence deserted. I stole across to the stable.

What if that groom had locked its door for the night? But no: he had been glad to delegate to me the task of caring for our animals, and doubtless was detained inside the tavern by this unusual press of company. The door hung ajar as I remembered to have left it.

I dared not attract possible attention by leaving it save as I found it, so that the stable was very dark. Nevertheless, early lessons in neatness had taught me always to put things where they could readily be found again; I knew precisely where saddles and bridles had been bestowed and so could have speeded my work blindfolded.

"Brave Success!" I whispered, as I patted my stallion. "Good Corsair! We can't rest to-night. We must start out again."

With burning fingers, I set about doing what I had undone on our arrival. The horses stood like soldiers under my orders. Once I risked a few seconds to steal to the door and listen: a light shone from our apartment, but the deepening shadows of the court were deserted; in the tap-room that low growl of narrative rumbled on.

Back to my work I went. I hesitated to make the girths tight so soon after a feeding; I made them as tight as I dared. Why did Sir Geoffrey not come? Both Success and Corsair opened their mouths for the bit. They were ready now, yet I dreaded the noise of hoofs on cobbles: I did not want to lead them out until Sir Geoffrey was come.

Again I tiptoed into the yard. The tap-room narrator reached his history's climax. His voice rose; its final words cleft the night:

"And they are in this tavern now!"

There burst a jangle of metal: the speaker had slapped a mug-laden table with his angry fist, and the pewter rattled.

Quick as echo, his hearers—or it must have been those of them who were village loafers, to whom the tale was new—broke into shouts. There were calls of " Where —where? " There was a choral summons for the host and waiter, and above it all there rose one hateful shriek:

" Spies! " And again " Spies! " And yet again: " Pennsylvania spies! "

Behind the window of Sir Geoffrey's room the light went out.

Booted feet rushed madly up a stair. I ran back to the stable. No need for quiet now: boldly, I led the willing horses into the yard. I hurried to the gate: this was no repetition of Lancaster; all was well here, the portal swung open to the street.

Unperturbed by the thunder from the inn, those splendid animals had not moved, but no sooner was I returned to them than a tremendous hubbub broke above. The Marylanders had reached Sir Geoffrey's room.

A door smashed. A clatter of glass and breaking furniture resounded as the intruders stumbled in. Two shots were fired almost as one. My eyes strained toward that window behind which I had left Sir Geoffrey. It was flung wide.

Then, from the carefully upraised neighoring casement, a figure leaped. About it there spread out, like a sail, the folds of a vast cloak: Sir Geoffrey, at the shout of " Spies! " had left his own room, locked behind him, but empty, and stolen into the next, which he rightly guessed to have been temporarily quitted by its occupant for the pleasure of the bar.

It was a trick worthy of its inventor, but, having delayed until the last possible instant its execution, out of a desire to give me every moment for my preparations that could be spared, it necessitated too much haste in its final phase. Sir Geoffrey should have wrapped his cape about him; he was too hurried to think of that; as he leaped, its folds must have caught one of his spurs: he twisted and struck the cobbles with a thud that sickened me.

I ran to him. The other window-space was spotted with faces. Sir Geoffrey tried to rise. He sank back with what, in the darkness, I could just make out to be a crooked smile.

" My pesky leg," said he: " the left. 'Tis broke, Nicky."

The faces above us yelled oaths. The flames of pistols spat. I heard the lead beat on the cobbles: only the darkness saved us. That sharp pattering of lead on the stones almost unnerved me.

" Go down! " That was surely the ferret calling. " Into the courtyard and after them! "

Sir Geoffrey caught my arm. "You must leave me, lad. Mount and ride—for your life."

"I won't go alone," said I.

His anger flared. "You'll obey orders!"

I disobeyed them. How I accomplished it, I know not, but, heavy as he was and badly as it hurt him, I lifted him bodily in my arms and set him in his saddle.

Again boots battered on the stairs—but this time they were descending.

"You must hang on by one leg," said I.

The thing being accomplished, he dropped his air of an officer. "But I'll faint from pain, like a very woman, I will."

I sprang astride Success. "Then I'll lash you fast as soon as there's the chance."

The door from the inn jumped open.

"Now!" I cried—and we clattered into the empty street.

A volley followed us.

"Are you hit?" I called.

I heard his welcome "No"—and then everything was gulped up by the pounding of our horses' hoofs.

The houses flew past. Out of them, with confusing blasts of light, cottagers ran to see what meant the noise, but not till we had reached the end of the village and were come well past it, to a fork in the road, could I hear another word from my companion.

Physical agony was in his voice, but also a spirit un-defeated:

"Not north, Nicky: we will not yet retreat. Turn south, my lad—turn south!"

CHAPTER XXX

THROUGH A TENT-FLAP

ALL night we rode, pausing only to lash Sir Geoffrey to his saddle and, against his protests, to give him such ease as I could from the pain he endured. He did not faint, as he had feared he might, but he suffered cruelly. I urged the seeking of another settlement and inquiry for a physician there: he had, however, recovered his authority, said such a course would surrender us into the hands of the enemy, and steadfastly persisted that, though we left the highroad for less dangerous ways, we should head in no direction save a southerly.

At the start, this advice which seemed so close to foolhardy did, I think, save us. Ferret-face and his fellows had to saddle ere they could pursue; they could ask for us to the village-end, but, thence onward to the forks of the road, there were no houses at which to make inquiries: they must then have assumed that, our mission discovered, we should seek a return to Pennsylvania, and most like they did not detect their mistake until immediate capture was impossible.

Cold dawn found us in a nest of rocky hills, and, turning abruptly among these and riding across country, we began to search for some hiding-place. Houses were again few, the narrow valleys were largely natural meadows, but the woods were thick. I explored one forest afoot, found what seemed a promising asylum, with some chance of leading our horses thither, and this I eventually accomplished.

I helped Sir Geoffrey to dismount and inquired as to his leg.

"Oh, 'tis probably no break, after all," said he, and would not let me touch it; but he all but fell to the ground, and was white, with his face very drawn.

We were in a little depression half-way up a hillside. For the horses there was grass from which the day's progress tardily banished the rime, and we had the food that was in my companion's cape. Our dell was protected from the wind, but open to such rain or snow as might fall. The place was sufficiently concealed, yet clearly untenable for any length of time. You may imagine, then, my consternation when, after a short sleep, I woke to find Sir Geoffrey in a high fever and regretfully admitting that he could not mount a horse for many a week to come.

"Then," said I, "your leg *is* broken?"

"Fetch me some wood," said he. "I must whittle splints, or I shall be the first Faulkner to wear a crooked leg."

When I returned with this, he was cutting strips from his cloak's edge to bind the splints with. He was a man that loved his clothes, and this went hard with him. At my proffer to hack away his boot, I thought he would have whipped me; with twisted lips and sweating brow, he sat silent while I drew the leather off him.

Then he began again at me to leave him.

" What, when you cannot even forage for yourself? " I asked.

He said he would make shift somehow.

" You could not," said I, " and if you persist in such talk, I shall leave you only to bring a physician with me."

" You are a poor soldier," he grumbled.

" If I deserted my commander, I should be," said I.

He argued; he stormed. I let him wear himself out and then inquired of him what there was to be gained by my going. Without listening for his answer, I told him brutally that, so long as I kept out of reach of his arms, he was in my power, and that, reason as he might, I was determined to have my own way. I think it was my reiterated threat of a doctor that finished him.

" Poof! " said he: " a broken leg more or less! What's that? I can do all a surgeon could. Why, I learnt the trick during my first campaign, in the Low Countries, and I have since performed it on others a score of times."

So between us, we put his poor limb upon the rack. Though he would not complain of the torture, it served to quiet him in regards to me, and he only infrequently thereafter, and then in moments of natural dejection, reverted to the project of my abandoning him.

The cold remains of that supper, which he had carried away with him from the inn, lasted us a full week, and the horses, unexercised, did well enough on the sweet grasses of our refuge. These conditions could not, however, indefinitely continue: the time came when I had tremblingly to fare forth and seek not the nearest, but a more distant, crossroads store, where I bought some supplies and two pair of blankets, under a pretense of being a newly-arrived servant at a not too closely neighboring farm.

Then, as the weather grew both colder and inclement, with first some chilly rain and thereafter a light fall of snow, I made successful search for a better shelter, finding another dell higher up the hill and, in its limestone sides, a dry and not uncomfortable cave. A little housecleaning made this a really decent place of residence, and at its mouth I built a stove of stones, so that the glow of the fire would be hidden, and did all our cooking by night, when the smoke could not be visible in the distant valley. Sir Geoffrey's campaigning and his generally adventurous existence had given him more than a smattering of many arts: lying helpless, he yet directed me in the preparation of food and told me how to procure some of what we required by the building of snares and the setting of them.

So did the time drag itself along into a depth of

winter, with my patient mending very slowly from what must have been an evil fracture, but never losing ground. As often as I must, I left him to supplement our food-supply—for game grew scarce as the cold increased—by visits to distant stores, and in one day I got and hauled away on the back of good Success enough grain to serve that stallion and Corsair for a long time to come. Nevertheless, our clothes were in a dire condition, and, since I feared to visit any store more than twice, our position became more and more precarious.

We existed in a constant dread of discovery. Ultimate inquiry must have proved that we had not escaped into Pennsylvania by the highroad, and escape through the forest must have appeared unlikely, so that our continued presence between the proper boundaries of Maryland was, we believed, held as sure by any within whose interest it lay to seek us. The thing that saved us—the diverting preparations that I was later to discover—we did not yet guess, and Sir Geoffrey (who made his major time pleasant for me with further reminiscences of his European adventures, improved my French and even grounded me in Latin) began to devote more and more of his leisure to scolding himself for inveigling me on what he now freely condemned as a fool's errand.

I knew that he was, like myself, secretly distressed by conjectures as to what might be going forward at

" Lynton "; and that he feared lest Mr. Wright should think us mere lying rogues who had broken their parole. The better he grew, the more my invalid fretted at the inevitable inaction; he counted over and over the days that must still wall him in, and now condemned himself as an old woman and again criticized me sharply for the most trifling lapses.

Week followed week. One slow month dragged by, and the half of another. You are to picture us often snowed in, heating ice to procure water, sharing our cave with our horses, and mostly more hungry than were they. Now I got food or fodder, from one place, then from another, but not infrequently all journeying forth was impossible. Sir Geoffrey tried to walk a few steps and could not; his long autobiography exhausted itself, and his short patience with it. He alternated between fits of temper and the singing of " The Lass O' Morven " over and over again, until, much as I had loved it on a time, I came near to hating that tear-wringing melody; yet all the while he kept his torso limber and his arms strong by constant exercising of them while in a sitting posture, and I exercised the animals as best I could. Then came a day when my companion was able to hobble a few steps, and I had all that I could do to prevent a dangerous overexertion.

About this time, the weather somewhat ameliorating, I had a scare at one of the stores I visited. Whether or no the proprietor suspected me I am now in doubt, but he questioned me as to my identity in a manner that then quite frightened me, and, having got safe away from him, I thereafter secured supplies only by stealing them from outlying farms, and much annoyed Sir Geoffrey by an insistence on money to leave behind me in payment for what I could find.

" This is war," he complained, " and invaders must live off the country."

Nevertheless, he was ever the more tender of my scruples the less he shared in them. Out of his apparently inexhaustible purse, we paid our way in this odd manner, and I can conjecture only that the wildness of the country and its inhabitants' preoccupation with more pressing matters prevented a proper search for the strange thieves that pestered them.

Then at last appeared one of those unseasonable thaws to which this section of America is so liable. We had spring-like days that melted everything, and Sir Geoffrey's leg mended amazingly. He declared himself completely cured; he was, indeed, nearly so, and he was increasedly determined to move. That evening being very overcast and dark, I set out on a foraging-expedition and discovered something to our great advantage.

I resolved to go far, for I feared the nearer neighborhood must be now on the alert against my continued depredations, and I had of late observed, in a northerly direction, an activity that pricked my curiosity. For more than a fortnight, groups of men had been riding up the highway and into another valley, and almost none rode back. I thought I would seek food in that quarter, and I hoped to find information.

Find it I did.

For ten miles and more I skirted the road, passing first between the hills and finally coming, by late dark, to a wide plain. I rounded a hillock and found myself at the edge of a rude military camp.

There was no mistaking its nature. Tents were pitched, fires burning and sentries pacing to and fro. They wore a sort of irregular uniform, and from a drill-ground in the centre of the cantonment an armed company was returning. The truth was instantly evident.

" This," I told myself, " is preparation for a determining armed invasion of Pennsylvania, that is to be the Marylanders' conclusive blow."

There and then, I resolved upon concluding my doubts. I would wait an opportunity, steal into the camp and procure what knowledge was obtainable of its numbers and armament.

For perhaps an hour, which seemed a certain dozen, I lay along a tree-limb and watched. The green train-bands went to their quarters. Supper was served, with floating smells that set my mouth awash; the guard was changed; the moon rose in silver, but was soon hid by heavy clouds; and then a lonely rider entered the compound and was, after due formality, escorted to a big tent at its heart that I understood must be that of the commanding officer.

I waited another fifteen or twenty minutes. Then I descended from my perch, crept to the confines of the camp and, lying flat on my belly, began to wriggle like a snake toward those headquarters. I had already some idea of the enemy's strength, but I was still hopeful of securing further information.

I had marked a point where the patrol passed only once in a long interval. Opposite it, I lay until a sentinel had walked along. No sooner was his back toward it than I scuttled forward and dropped flat again inside the lines.

Few people were stirring. I pushed forward, with my face scarce an inch above the wet turf. I squirmed on until I came to the rear of the commander's canvas residence. It was generously constructed and had a flap at the back. To this I lost no time in gluing my anxious ear.

All that was said came as clear to me as if no barrier intervened. Someone was giving information regarding the immediate Pennsylvania border-defenses, the lame plans of which had evidently been drawn up since our departure. He was indicating their several weaknesses—and his interlocutor addressed him as " Captain Cresap! "

I held my breath.

"So," pursued the informer, "where you should strike ——"

A sentry passed six yards behind me. I flattened myself closer against the ground. What next I heard was:

". . . Wright's Ferry, opposite Hempfield."

That other voice (the voice of the commander) asked: "Within four days?"

"Within four days," said the informer.

"Right, Captain Cresap. Here is the map. Is this the road?"

A mumbled assent answered him.

Only a strip of canvas hung between me and a sight of the mysterious Cresap. With shaking fingers I gingerly raised the flap and looked within and upward.

The interior of the tent was lighted by a pair of candles tilting from the tops of empty bottles placed on a table of unplaned boards. Between the candles lay several fresh road-maps, plainly the results of careful study, and over these was bent a pair of heads, the one black and of military cut, the other thin and sandy and, to my amazed gaze, shockingly familiar.

The man with the hair of military cut, who was in uniform, placed a stubby finger at a certain spot on one of the maps.

"They are to proceed by that road," said he, " and at this place "—the finger moved a little—" you will have a guide to meet us four days hence, at sunrise."

THROUGH A TENT-FLAP

" Very good, Colonel. I shall myself be that guide."

It was the man addressed as Cresap who made this reply: the man with the sandy hair. No other color of him could I then make out, for all but the top of his head was in shadow, yet even the shadow of him chilled me with partial recognition.

" And now," continued he, " with your permission, I must start on my return. I am quietly disposing of my Pennsylvania property, and must have that accomplished and be safe within your lines before you strike your blow."

" Very well." The Colonel's voice was crisp with a not uncertain scorn that reluctantly conceded something to curiosity as he added: " Your position under Thomas Penn has been a large one; the promised reward for your services against him must be—shall we say commensurate? "

A covetous laugh preceded the answer:

" There need be no longer any secret about it. Indeed, the sooner it is known by your forces, the better. Once the debated district has been securely occupied, the Proprietor of Maryland is to grant me two thousand of its best acres."

As he thus spoke, the traitor raised his head. There were only two men within the tent. The other had been addressed as " Colonel," this one as " Captain Cresap " —and this one was my step-uncle, Simon Scull!

CHAPTER XXXI

PERIL BY WATER

HOW shall I set down all that happened then? The thunder-stroke of recognition, when I was blasted by the truth that my step-uncle played both the Ranger of the Proprietor's Manor and its deadliest enemy—the swift return of sense, commanding conveyance of the news to Pennsylvania in time to raise a protective force against this planned invasion—the risky crawl back through the camp—the breathless rush across the forest—and the delivery of my tidings to Sir Geoffrey. So stunning was that which I had ascertained, and so pressing the peril, the memory of these things and of our subsequent journey from the cave in Maryland to the cave on Round Top is but a blur of mad impressions. Events befell with a rapidity that ran one upon another: I recall them only as one recalls a dream of the night.

"But this is what I guessed!" had cried Sir Geoffrey, when at last I staggered up with my revelation. "And this is what I hoped to find!"

"We have found it too late!" wailed I.

For how could we bring the news into Pennsylvania to make it of any use there? The ride must be a long one through a now suspicious country. With such a campaign afoot, the frontier would have been warned to watch for spies, and all the alarm of our affair at the inn would have been revived: we durst not ride by day, and every Maryland planter would have his eyes wide for a man and a boy that rode together. Meanwhile, Simon Scull, proceeding with proper credentials, would have gone ahead and perfected his treachery; certain it seemed that, even should we come through in safety and in advance of the soldiery, yet the Ranger would have made away with the jewels.

Nevertheless, there was no alternative.

"No man is dead until his heart stops beating," declared Sir Geoffrey. "I am well enough to ride: we must accomplish the impossible!"

What with weariness and despair, I was ready to drop; but my companion was no man to resist. All those hard weeks of winter lay upon me; already, this night, I had gone a score of miles afoot, yet was there no withstanding his energy or any failure of an able-bodied lad to follow where an invalid hesitated not to lead the way. He hobbled about his preparations; it was a matter of minutes only ere we were in saddle and away.

How we did the thing I know not, save by God's providence. We travelled in the darkness, hiding through the long, grudged hours of light. The steaming countryside stretched bare and naked about us; it lay silent, as if holding breath in expectation of approaching disaster; now and then dogs barked at our passage, but not once did we encounter anything human. That unseasonable warmth continued and increased, and it came on to rain heavily for twenty-four hours on end, so that not alone were we soaked to the skin, but the young roads were bogged, and progress very heavy.

We were half starved, but we were fortunate enough to have had a fair store of grain in our encampment: we provided, in our saddle-bags, travelling-space for the horses' food at the expense of it for ours, and so at least kept up the strength of our animals. Corsair never once fell below what was demanded, and as for my own Success, he appeared to comprehend our need and to understand the encouragement that I continuously called to him. We were to accomplish the impossible, and it was accomplished: recklessly toiling on the last half-day by gray daylight, we finally attained —a pair of ragged scarecrows—sight of the river-hills, and Round Top towering above all those to the north of the highway.

Not a living soul was to be seen. Sir Geoffrey turned into Anderson's Trail.

" That will not get us to ' Hempfield '! " I shouted.

Pushing right on, he flung his answer back at me:

" We must have Harley's report, or we may well be walking into a trap! "

Luckily, that curly-headed athlete was at home. We

had led our horses up a path, steep and almost untraceable, and there found him, a pistol drawn against inimical approach, before an outcropping of rock three-quarters up the hillside.

"What news?" asked Sir Geoffrey.

But he waited not upon the answer. Instead, we surrendered the horses—Success, at a word from me, going with Harley like a lamb—and Sir Geoffrey stopped to pass what at first appeared as only a low ledge of limestone.

I followed.

Immediately I was fronting a sturdy door. My friend opened it, and we descended some dozen precipitous steps, threaded a dark passage and came into a high, vaulted cavern, a circular, subterranean chamber perhaps thirty feet across.

You young people know it as a place where you have played at Roundhead and Cavalier, at Hessian and Continental; you have traced out the secrets of its draughts and ventilation; but you can never imagine its brief days of glory when the resourceful Harley had prepared it for what promised to be the long-housing of his master. Rugs covered the floor, secured I could not conjecture how; lamps hung from the natural ceiling of rock. There were even a rustic bed, table and chairs. A curtain that Sir Geoffrey drew aside revealed several hanging suits of clothes and an utterly incongruous mirror against the wall. Another opening in the rock disclosed a second room, evidently Harley's bedchamber and kitchen, and a fire was going there.

My host went to the wardrobe.

" Should we not hurry? " I ventured.

His dark face flashed me its handsome smile. " We are behind your good uncle, but that last dash must have brought us close enough after him to justify this pause. I choose to present myself to your Magistrate habited somewhat after the manner of a gentleman: clothes are convincing evidence. Nicky, look at your image and tell me if you would accept the accusation of such a villain! "

One glance in the mirror sufficed. I saw a long-haired, emaciated boy, clad in rags and caked with mud.

" Harley! " called Sir Geoffrey.

The man entered. He had shared a half of his master's adventurous career. I take it that sudden reappearances after inexplicably long absences were familiar to him. He bore himself as if we had left him in the turnip-field but yesterday.

" Those horses: you have cared for them? "

" Aye, Zur Geoffrey."

" Then food and news—quickly."

The marvellous servant hopped about his task and talked while he performed it. Bacon sizzled, and my mouth watered. The table was set as Sir Geoffrey and I were washing at a camp-washstand. My friend selected carefully a fresh suit and cloak for himself and

forced on me one that I made shift with by turning-up
of sleeves and breeches: fit there was little, but clothes
so fine had not touched me since I left Castle Wyke for
Squire Wedgewood's at Ayton.

" 'Tis better than rags," said Sir Geoffrey, surveying
me. He regarded his own likeness with more of approval. " And now we shall eat," he concluded.

By then, I needed no persuasion. I stuffed myself
on fat bacon and yellow eggs, and Harley's narrative
of events during our absence was brought down to the
present. It came to this:

Little Jacob had been spending most of his time on
the York County side of the river. It was clear that
Uncle Simon had information of the *contretemps* at
the inn, suspected that I was the boy in that case, and
was set upon laying me by the heels, through the Susquehannock's aid, should I attempt a return. On the
other hand, the Ranger himself had this afternoon appeared from the south and crossed the stream, which
was frozen, proceeding on horse over the ice. Now,
however, the ice had been breaking a few miles north; it
must already be unsafe opposite " Hempfield ": nobody
dared pass.

" Nobody? " repeated Sir Geoffrey. He had made
near as good a meal as me, and he laid down knife and
fork. " Why, as to that, this boy and I can, and you
must. We shall start this instant."

Nor, indeed, after our so deliberate preparations, did

we any further linger. Afoot, we cautiously descended the hill and, at sunset, came to a place on the shore directly opposite " Hempfield."

I was, I remember, in advance. I saw the figure of a massive man, hesitant before the vast sheet of ice that spread ahead of him. We had gone cautiously, but some slight sound indistinguishable to me now betrayed us. The figure turned, and I saw the fanged grin and one sightless rolling eye of Little Jacob.

My thought, if thought it may be called, was that he, having detected us, must be taken before he could cross the Susquehanna and warn Uncle Simon. I gave a great cry and plunged straight at him.

He saw that we were three to one, and he feared the ice. He leapt toward the river—dared not attempt it— wheeled and came headlong toward us as we spread out and ran forward.

I sprang right to his neck and hung there like a bull-dog. Sir Geoffrey seized one arm that held a pistol, and Harley grasped the other. We all went down in the mud.

Little Jacob fought like a tiger. His horrid teeth bit my cheek. He wrenched free of Harley. He delivered a mighty blow above me at Sir Geoffrey. As it went home, however, his hold of the pistol loosened, and my friend, though half-stunned by the Indian's fist, jerked free the weapon and pressed it to its owner's temple.

PERIL BY WATER

At once the struggle was over. Little Jacob surrendered.

"Well," he grunted, "where go?"

"With us," I gasped, pushing a handkerchief against my bleeding cheek.

"To the Magistrate's," supplemented Sir Geoffrey, "to lock you up on any charge we list and to denounce Master Scull as Captain Cresap."

The Susquehannock's whole eye roved toward the river. "How?"

He might well ask that. Through the gathering dusk, the ice stretched clear before us, well over a mile to the farther shore. Just here it looked secure enough, but less than five hundred yards up-stream was another picture. There the river's wintry armor, rusted by the rains, grew brown and gray and roughened. It rose in heaps; it showed wide seams and enlarging pools as our glances travelled northwards; it visibly heaved and then, beyond those clefts, it fell away completely and exposed a wide body of perturbed, lead-colored water. Even as Little Jacob spoke, there came from above a report as if a cannon was fired.

"He's right, zur," said Harley. "The ice here will be a-movin' in no time."

Sir Geoffrey shot his servant a single look. "We shall cross it."

"Very good, zur," said Harley.

The Susquehannock took his marching-orders in no

such spirit. He vowed that the attempt was certain death. He fought again. Again subdued, he fell on his knees and, in a panic-mixture of English and Indian, begged us to remain ashore. He slobbered; tears gushed alike from his good eye and its ghastly mate. I had enjoyed the moment of triumph over my former oppressor which came with his subjugation, but there is nothing more horrible than a bully's terror: my stomach revolted at this shameless exhibition of it.

Nevertheless, he had to go. Sir Geoffrey's pistol was at his head. There might be some small chance of survival in consent; in refusal there was not one.

And so we set out, the Indian first, his moccasined feet feeling every inch of the way, his knees knocking together; Sir Geoffrey next, with his weapon poised, and then Harley and I. The report so like to cannon was repeated with our progress—became louder—became continuous. In midstream, I could have sworn that I felt the ice heave under me. We came to cracks. We came to chasms that we vaulted and pools that we circled—and that widened as we circled them. We went in silence, and our best speed became too slow. Increasing danger enveloped us; it gathered around us in a thickening mist that rose from the ice and a burthening darkness that dropped from the skies. We could feel death stirring, yet we could not see a furlong on either hand.

I think that we all welcomed the end of this, the open

attack that seemed the end of us as well. There was a series of explosions, and then a loud rending noise. Thirty yards from shore we were when the ice rose and tore asunder beneath us; great slabs tilted upward into hills—ground together—crushed and fell—and there was each man separately afloat on a tossing floe.

Sir Geoffrey flung away the pistol. He turned to help me—a gulf of rapid water yawned between us, black and hopeless.

Followed a space of mad action that outdistanced thought. We had but one emotion; our sole instinct was to save our lives. We hopped from floe to yielding floe, our arms outflung to keep a desperate balance, our feet slipping, the upsplashing water chilling our sweating bodies; but the Susquehannock's lead and training gave him the best advantage: he reached the bank first and ran toward " Lynton," a free man once more.

What happened to the others I do not know. I know that twice I nearly fell; I know that an ice-cake to which I sprang turned and submerged me—that I struck out to swim—that another floe struck me—that I thrust wide my arms, and that then, from the shore, Sir Geoffrey and Harley were hauling me in.

" So after all," said the former, " our careful toilets were wasted. And now for ' Hempfield.' "

I coughed the water from my mouth. " No—no! After him! " I choked.—" After Little Jacob! He's off to warn Uncle Simon, and they'll have joined the Mary-landers before ——"

But already Sir Geoffrey was speeding toward " Hempfield," which rose in front of us. He made a motion backward. Words were not needed to explain that gesture: no man could here cross the Susquehanna now. The Ranger must escape some other way; his junction with the Marylanders, at least by this part of the river, was effectually barred.

CHAPTER XXXII

" GUNS! "

OUR agitated knocking's answer was Mr. Wright himself unbarring the door. Thomas, Shawanese survivor of the turnip-field fray, stood beside him; behind, in the square hall, what I surmised to be the rest of the " Hempfield " household gathered. Out of their caverns, the Magistrate's eyes flashed as Sir Geoffrey, in less than threescore of words, reported, and I added the bare fact of what I had seen on the Joppa Trail.

" He'll ride down-stream to seek solid ice! " cried the Quaker.

No doubting of our accusation, you observe, nor waste of precious instants by cross-questioning. Proof must wait upon capture: Wright, in a crisis, was a man of action.

" Either that, or we shall catch the fox in his hole," said Sir Geoffrey. " I'm hoping his servant thinks we drowned in the river."

The Magistrate was twitching with suppressed indignation. Right and left, he flung orders. He interrupted himself only to jerk out:

265

"Then, if we surprise the rogue, he will defend himself. He has his own sort of courage."

"'Twas why I came here first," explained my companion: "not fear of losing my life, but dread of losing, through superior numbers, our proper prisoners."

The Magistrate was not heeding. "Guns, Thomas! There, thee knows: in the closets beside the fireplace! —By Heaven's decree, Patterson is in our kitchen this moment, and some of his men with him: call them, James, and give them the news!—Thee, Prince"— this to an Indian servant—"all the horses, and don't thee stop to saddle them!—The Lord Proprietary is making his semi-annual tour of the Province; he should have been here two hours since. If he has not stopped for the night at the courthouse, he should reach 'Hempfield' ere dawn.—Leave word that he be sent on, should he come in our absence."—The Quaker beat his palms together as a rider cracks his whip.—"Where is that negro, Peter?—Peter, scour the settlement and bid the folk to 'Lynton'!"

Someone—it was one of the younger Wrights—asked what charge we should lodge against Scull. The Magistrate turned on him in a towering scorn:

"The murder of Knowles Daunt! That will serve to hold him—and this lad is our witness."

He pushed through the door. We followed.

"One warning," he continued, and I noted that a wind had sprung up so brisk as to flutter his broad-

brimmed hat: " If we do not meet him on the way, surround the house; then there must be no violence until
the law is resisted."

The horses clattered 'round. Patterson and his men
followed. Guns were tossed to us. Our mounts were
bridled only; through the deepening twilight, we rode
bareback to " Lynton."

Little Jacob must indeed have reported us as probably drowned, and the Ranger, though preparing to escape against the chance of our rescue, had yet been more
leisurely than if his Susquehannock had stopped to see
us make our way ashore. In the thickening shadows of
its lawn and topped only by the single oak, " Lynton "
stood gray and silent, the doors closed, the lower windows shuttered; but from the casement in that attic,
where the master of the house must be getting his papers together, one dim light shone.

We had covered the last part of the way as quietly
as might be. Arrived, we tethered our horses beneath the roadside pines. Then Wright dispersed
his forces and started to walk alone toward the front-
door.

" That is dangerous," Sir Geoffrey cautioned and
would have accompanied him.

" Stand back! " said Wright. " I am King's Magistrate here, and I know my duty."

He knocked.

There came no answer.

" Simon Scull," he cried in a ringing voice, " open, in the name of the law! "

The sound of it was like a shot. The mullioned attic-window was flung wide, and a face peered out. With the light behind it, I could not distinguish the features, but the tones that issued with it were the tones of the Ranger, high and thin:

" Is it thee, Friend? "

" Come down and open! " Wright demanded. " Your house is encompassed; resistance will be useless! "

I saw a shadow pass behind the challenged householder. He temporized:

" And what is all this about the law to the Ranger of the Proprietor's Manor? Where does thee keep that law? At home? No citizen's house is liable to trespass without due warrant." Another head and shoulders bent out now beside the speaker's: Little Jacob was there. " Has thee a warrant, Friend John? "

Wright's patience broke:

" I had the warrant of my suspicions; I have the corroboration of thy delay. I am come to arrest thee for the murder of Knowles Daunt, and unless this door be straightway opened ——"

I truly think that Simon Scull, if only from caution and the hope that delay might bring some means of escape, disapproved the Susquehannock's purpose. I surmise that Little Jacob had been warming himself with fire-water against the chill of his river-crossing. Certainty there is none. All that I surely know is that the Ranger made a gesture of dissent—and made it too late. Out of that window, the Indian fired on the Magistrate.

The shot failed. Wright raised his head, and his grotesquely nautical pigtail stuck out behind it.

That was our signal. From those of us on the front lawn, a half-dozen rifles spurted toward the attic casement; but our bullets merely buried themselves in some piece of furniture that had been instantaneously pushed there, and, from the slit between this and the open sash, flashes of fire answered. The Indian Thomas dropped at my side.

" Storm the house! " Wright shouted.

And from every angle, our forces flung themselves upon " Lynton."

On barred doors and bolted shutters rained the fury of our gun-butts. From the attic, the shots of two pistols fell, and brought down one more of our party: the Ranger, driven to desperation, was loading and firing by the Susquehannock's side.

It developed that the Shawanese servants of my stepuncle were not among the defenders, but cowered in their own outlying huts, unwilling to aid their master, yet too much in fear of him to aid the law. Nevertheless, the giantess Massáya was there, fighting for the love of it; she ran from one second-story window to another, and she, having the eyes of a cat, near every time she levelled her rifle, she levelled a member of our posse with the ground.

The wind increased. Nothing save the flashes of explosions lightened the darkness, at last intense, and we shot rather from blind instinct than from sight. On the stout barrier of the house we might as well have been beating with bare fists, whereas the exposure of our positions gave our enemies at least shadows to aim at and so was resulting in heavy harm.

"Fall back!" the Magistrate ordered those immediately about him, in which number Sir Geoffrey and I labored, and Harley also. "To the stable, young Rowntree, and fetch an axe. Fell a tree in the woods: we must have a battering-ram for this work!"

"If we all fall back," objected Sir Geoffrey, "the villain will jump and run for it."

That one of Wright's sons whom I have already mentioned solved our difficulty. He came tearing from an outhouse, an axe ready in his hand.

"This alone," he cried when he understood our arguments, "will serve the kitchen-door, and over it is no window for them to shoot from!"

"Does thee have sufficient men there?" his father demanded.

"Quite."

"Then guard we this side, lest the fellow leap."

Sir Geoffrey was for joining the party that would

enter. I saw him motion Harley to remain with the
Magistrate. Then my friend slipped through the dark-
ness toward the kitchen, and I slipped stealthily after.
We heard the axe fall; we heard wood splinter. Sir
Geoffrey grasped my arm:

"Look—look!"

One end of the shingle-roof flaunted a tongue of
flame that was like a yellow plume. Swinging himself
from the old oak in the rear, the Irishman Patterson—
I knew him by the shape of his coonskin cap—had
gained that post of vantage and started a conflagration.
We two alone saw him clamber back to the tree and
descend thence to the turf.

Scattered settlers, roused by the negro Peter, were
straggling up, more wondering than useful. Shots
rang out; the axe rose and fell, and up above, known as
yet to but three of us, the snake-tongued ally advanced
our cause. The wind was high, the rain that had irked
Sir Geoffrey and me on the last stage of our journey
to Round Top had not crossed the river; the shingles
were dry fodder for the blaze.

A blaze it immediately became, and so our whole
company were aware of it. Light bathed them. They
lifted their gaping heads—and then lifted the frighten-
ing cry of "Fire!"

CHAPTER XXXIII

FIRE!

UP from the river the wind blew yet stronger. Across the roof of " Lynton " danced a ballet of orange sparks that widened where they fell. They rose in flames and broke of a sudden into a gluttonous roar.

The oaken barrier to the kitchen had crashed down to the blows of James Wright's axe, but the men around it stood rooted there and renewed that cry of " Fire! " —only now the word was one of exultation and not alarm. They realized their work was being done for them; they need but wait that inevitable moment when the elemental demon must drive the murderer into their ready arms.

" Well," says Sir Geoffrey to me, " this eases matters." And he made toward the group.

I guessed what occupied all his mind: the recovery of the jewels, which he had perhaps begun to fear he might not see until they fell into the hands of King George's officers. Those gems, since their return to the Stuarts touched my father's honor, were as much my concern as his: I went close after him.

He shouldered smartly among the men at the door.

272

One guessed that he had some mad project of entering and would have restrained him.

At that, I jumped around the pair. Unnoted, I scuttled inside the house.

"Unhand me!" I heard Sir Geoffrey say. "And do not follow: I have a right to take this prisoner."

He must have won compliance, for he was well-nigh at once beside me in the kitchen.

"So you are in here?" he asked, and then said he: "Perhaps it is as well; I may require help."

There was a kettle of cold water there. He dipped a lace handkerchief in it.

"Put this over your nose and into your mouth," he said. "See: I shall knot it at the base of your neck, for we may run into the flames." To his own protection, he drew his cloak tighter around him and the upper folds above his chin. "Pistols," he concluded and, his own in his hand, led the way.

We crossed the dining-room,—my companion had been walking with scarce a limp. When we reached the hall, a cloud of smoke came rolling slowly down the stairs.

Into that we plunged. Upon the first landing, a door opened and showed the evil face of Massáya.

Swiftly as Sir Geoffrey ever acted, he never moved more quickly than he did then: she had no chance to shoot. With one bound he was at her; his pistolled hand shoved her back into the room whence she had been peeping; his other transferred the key from the inside to the outside of the lock: he locked her in.

She beat upon the panels. She screamed.

"That proves there is but this sole door to her room," said Sir Geoffrey, nodding against the noise. "No rear attack on us, then. We can release her as we return down-stairs."

Two steps at a time, three good legs and one newly mended, we hurried up the remaining flight. The smoke thickened; like a wall it was. The air lashed my cheeks and stung my eyes. Something as if a volley of shots assailed our ears: the crackling of flames.

The attic-door stood ajar; we ran in. Under a tossing canopy of fire, crouched the Ranger and Little Jacob, the former clutching the smaller of his two precious boxes in his skinny arms.

I suppose our entrance was itself terrible. One of us dripped from the river, and his bitten cheek was brown with blood; both of us were wet with the sweat of our haste. My companion's handkerchief concealed my face's lower half; his own hid in his cloak. The pair held pistols, and, Sir Geoffrey's plumes singeing at the flames above, he shook off his hat, and his long black curls fell about his flushed cheeks and marked out his eyes that shone inexorable triumph.

Nevertheless, however we looked, the look of the Ranger and his Susquehannock I shall never forget.

Little Jacob's figure stooped from that overhanging

cloud of fire. His shirt was gone, and the skin shone
like burnished copper-armor moulded to his bulging
muscles and knobby chest. The matted hair fell across
his low forehead; his grin was fixed; his horrible fangs
snarled, and, though his good eye was cruel, the blind
one rolled yet more evilly, like a thing of independent
and twice-malignant life.

There is repulsiveness in wicked strength; there is
more in wicked craft, and of that the always bent form
of Simon Scull presented now a perfect personification.
He was wearing his old garments of the color of iron-
rust, and only then did I understand how well they
suited him: the brown of a loathsome beetle—the brown
of a sewer-rat at bay.

His long, pale countenance had a smudge of powder
or soot across it, beginning at his left cheek-bone and
bridging his vulturine nose to the left-hand corner of
his champing mouth. His red-rimmed eyes were
bleared in their corners alone; from the sockets' centres
the pinhead pupils raged balefully, and he held that
treasure-box in his claws with just the grip wherewith,
when I had first seen him, in the Delaware, he grasped
the boat that he feared might capsize.

So poised the pair of my enemies. The fire cracked
above them; it lapped down at them with a hundred
greedy tongues; around them bellied what seemed the
smoke of the Pit, and it was an awesome thing thus
to observe these two, so different and yet both so dia-

bolic, grinning at us, each in his own specially infernal way.

I say that I can never forget this, and yet, as Satan revealed the world from the mountain, I saw it all for only a moment of time. In that veritable furnace, the loose boards were still turning under our approach as the ice-floes had turned under us on the river, when Scull freed one hand, flinging it up in a motion of surrender—and with that the Susquehannock raised his pistol and fired.

Sir Geoffrey shot from the hip, but he shot first. One blast was indistinguishable from the other, yet there my friend remained uninjured, and Little Jacob, for the sake of the one man he feared and the only being he loved—and him a villain—lay dead at my feet.

" Hold Scull! " yelled Sir Geoffrey.

I swung mad hands upon the Ranger. There came a resounding crash from the landing, but I heeded it not: I was embracing my cursing captive while he, in a mania of desperation, fought like a wildcat.

He fought in vain. Sir Geoffrey had the box and then had its keys (for a fresh lock had been fitted to it) from the Ranger's writhing person.

" So much for your indenture! " cried my champion.

Out of the box he plucked the falsely-contrived paper that had sought to make a slave of me. He tore it across and tossed it upward, and the burning ceiling swallowed it aflame.

FIRE!

I saw him stuff handfuls of jewels into his shirt; but Simon Scull's wriggling body, his snapping mouth and clawing nails held more than half my attention. He fought—I must grant him so much credit—through the last red instant of hope.

" Enough! "

It was Sir Geoffrey's shout. I loosed my hold.

We turned to the door by which we had entered—the only door from the attic. Over the landing there the roof had fallen: a fort of flame barred our exit.

CHAPTER XXXIV

A FRIEND INDEED

FIVE minutes more in that attic would be death. "Help!" bawled Simon Scull.

Except to curse us, it was the first articulate word he had uttered since our entrance.

Flames advanced on us from the doorway, and flames reached down from the rafters to welcome them. Sparks fell. Patches of flooring began to smoulder. The leggins of the dead Indian at our feet were already charred. The heat blistered us; the whirling smoke made breathing at once a danger and an agony. We two avengers and the miserable creature whom we had just desperately despoiled of his plunder were drawn together like blood-brothers on a single oasis in that desert of fire.

Sir Geoffrey pointed to the window. Speech he would not risk; none was required. He meant: "Jump!"

The Ranger's terror of burning forgot suffocation's perils. "We can't!" he screamed, and then half strangled from the smoke.

It seemed that he was right. Somewhere behind the coming sheet of flame was that other window: the window that was broken on the night of the autumnal thun-

der-storm. Glaziers were then few and glass a rarity
in these parts; though the miser had had a new lock
fitted to his treasure, the broken window was not repaired, and from it a draft now fanned the bottom of
the lambent sheet forward, across the flooring and out
of the attic-casement, whence, in the zeal of rapid
marksmanship, the erstwhile blockading piece of furniture must have been some time since dragged away. To
jump from there, we must first dive into a running
stream of flame. Up at us the lifeless mouth of Little
Jacob grinned derisively.

And yet we did escape. Sir Geoffrey pushed me to
the casement.

" Do we not always leave houses thus? " he cried.

The sill burnt my hands. I let go: I did not drop;
I leaped—and somehow I landed safely on my feet before the group of watchers, almost at John Wright's
knees. As he helped me rise, and Harley ran up with
a tardy horse-blanket, Sir Geoffrey alighted after me.
I expected that he would refracture his newly-healed
leg, but he lighted on its fellow, and though he at once
toppled over, he came to the ground safely: in his arms
was the Ranger, nor was there a single bone broken
among us all.

" Hold this prisoner! His lieutenant is dead! "

My friend tossed Simon into the anxious grasp of
Patterson. Another crash came from within, and then
a piercing shriek: we had forgotten Massáya!

The fall of that portion of the roof above the attic-landing must have fired the floor below. We could see gusts of flame behind its windows. Glass burst and tinkled on the ground, and the burning arms reached forth into the night as if they lusted to consume the world. A series of shocking wails rode out on them.

" I must save her! "—Sir Geoffrey started forward.

Protesting hands were laid on him—among them even the usually well-disciplined Harley's. Men cried that the resolve was madness—that it came too late—that nobody was to blame—and that Massáya deserved her punishment. The arguments he did not answer; the hands he flung off. He struggled to the kitchen-door, but thence a blast of smoke too violent for human endurance drove him back. He tried again and was driven out with his face and hair singed and his clothes afire.

" A ladder! " he called. " There must be a ladder in the barn! "

His heroic determination dragged with him those who most disapproved its object—even those who most dreaded to share its endeavor. We got the thing we sought.

As we bore it toward the house, an entire window-frame fell from the room in which we had locked Massáya. Back of it roared a veritable furnace, and at the yawning mouth she herself appeared, her face scarce human, the very snake-locks of her hair in flame.

Every countenance among the besiegers was turned

280

gaping up toward her, and each became, in the red light, a picture of consternation.

"Wait! Wait!" called some.

"Jump!" called others.

Perhaps she had been too dazed to jump before, or too fearful of her reception; perhaps some high savage pride, which could not silence her shrieks, had yet compelled her to wait death behind a door that defied even her strength, rather than cravenly leap from an open window to surrender. Our approach I doubt if she could now see; I doubt if she could hear our contrary commands; but the access of physical pain must have shattered whatever had been her inhibitions. Before we reached the house, she had thrown herself headlong from it.

During the merest quiver of an eyelid, she flew downward, a flaming body. When we got to her, she was as dead as Little Jacob.

One look sufficed me: the woman had been no friend to my loneliness, yet what she now was passed, it seemed, all justice. I was burnt and bruised and wellnigh broken; that night had been filling me with horrors, and this one overflowed my capacity. I staggered away a few paces, unobserved. Beside a bush, I lay down, and I think I must have fainted. When I looked up again, the whole of "Lynton" was one bonfire. Its light illuminated the lawn, and thither something drew my gaze.

THE RANGER OF THE SUSQUEHANNOCK

At the gate, Simon Scull was on his knees, his Quaker pose forgot, but yammering in broad Yorkshire speech for mercy. Over him stood Mr. Wright with—as I observed on drawing close—the expression of a prosecuting attorney. Around, on foam-flecked horses, sate a number of men that included wiry Constable Jones, the cheek-scarred half-breed Chance and the stomachy trader Cartlidge, who all, through everything which followed, remained almost as statues out of their tall respect for him who had the centre place among them, his regular features as rigidly composed as on the only other occasion that I had seen him: Thomas Penn, the Lord Proprietor.

The formal accusation of Scull as the assassin of Knowles Daunt had already been made; the Ranger's identity with Thomas Cresap was practically admitted; the plans of the Marylanders stood revealed. Penn, with an infinite calm, was announcing his decision.

He said that he would at once raise a defending force. He would send word to the Calverts that their troops would be met by superior numbers, and that they must therefore recognize the safety of the theory which he himself had ever maintained: decent reference of the whole boundary-dispute to the Court of Chancery in London.

"And I shall add," said he, smiling ever so little, "that, if this be not done, why, whatever the issue of battle, the charge of murder against Baltimore's chief agent, this Cresap, will be pressed to the point of capital punishment ——"

From his knees, Simon Scull set up another howl—and abhorrently I felt again on my hands the touch of the gallows-steps that I had experienced in Lancaster.

" Or else," continued Penn, raising one of his well-cared-for hands, " to the point of securing from thee, poor wretch, a sworn confession necessarily involving so many of Calvert's supporters in irregularities that any court in England will throw out their claims."

Like a mere slit across his tallow face with its smudge of soot, the Ranger's mouth worked spasmodically. In a very transport of terror, he spread wide his arms.

" I'll swear—ah, ban, I will thot! I'll tell 't all! " A strange soul: forced to fight, he had fought without honor, yet without fear; compelled to implore, he as recklessly flung away all conscience and all shame. " You've shown how t'end t'war! " He wriggled forward to the Proprietor's stump. " Only spare my life, and I'll gie you t'name of every Maryland conspirator. Oh, spare my poor life! "

I saw Penn's lip curl. Little as the Ranger deserved mercy, it was upon me—with the memory of that gallows—to plead for him, when Sir Geoffrey appeared from behind the Constable, where he seemed to have been speaking with Harley, who now walked away to-

ward the horses that had brought us from " Hempfield."
His master whispered long and privately with Wright
and Penn. Thereafter spoke the last of these:

" Simon Scull, if we save further warfare through
thy confession, why, though thee must leave this Commonwealth, thy life is safe."

The Ranger caught his hand and kissed it. Penn
drew it back. He dismounted and beckoned me a few
steps apart.

Being grown now, I understand the purport of what
he told me there in the light of flaming " Lynton " as
well as you know how the border-dispute did indeed go
to the Court of Chancery and was settled in Penn's
favor. The Ravenscar fortune had passed to Scull only
as part of my father's punishment on the charge of
treason to the so-called King George: if my father received a certain sort of royal pardon, his fortune would
revert to him. Well, at that talk with Sir Geoffrey in
the hut on the turnip-field, Mr. Wright had promised
to secure, through Penn, just such a pardon, should we
bring about the arrest of the man, then but suspected,
who had been betraying the Pennsylvanians' plans to
the Marylanders. This, in the capture of Simon Scull,
we had to-night accomplished: the legal technicalities
were not at once clear to me, but the Lord Proprietary
made it evident that I could look forward with certainty
to my father's enrichment and release.

Overcome with joy, I saw yet some difficulties. " I

know he is not like my step-uncle: he will not betray
his friends!"

"He will not be asked to do so," Penn smilingly assured me. "But he is no longer young, and the very
master that he has served so well will consent to his
honorable discharge from that service and his settlement
in this Colony. There are ways of finding these
things out, and we have found them. Nay, while you
have been absent, matters have been tentatively ar-
ranged even, as we hope, to your brave father's satisfaction."

I tried to utter my thanks. My eyes caught my
friend's.

"But Sir Geoffrey!" I cried, ashamed for my for-
getfulness. "The Whigs hate him also. What will
happen to Sir Geoffrey Faulkner?"

Mr. Penn bent to me. "I am growing a little deaf,
my lad. I did not catch the gentleman's name.—No,
thee need not repeat it. Magistrate Wright and I know
only that he has been most useful: I think, however,
that if he modestly disappears, we shall not make search
for him to reward him."

"But," I began, "he ——" And there I stopped
short, remembering the true purpose of Sir Geoffrey's
mission in America.

Thomas Penn turned back to the circle of officers.
In their midst, Simon Scull had risen, on his smudged
and pimpled face a smirk of satisfaction: he had saved

his life; he held information of value; he was once more a person of importance.

"And so, Friend Simon," said Penn to him, "because of thy promised confession, which will prevent further bloodshed, and because the sole witness to thy—shall we call it 'fight'?—thy fight with Knowles Daunt is a relative who, I believe, would be loath to hang thee through his testimony—because of these things, thy skin is safe—but not thy lands."

Never did expression change more rapidly than Simon Scull's. His red eyes stared, his long jaw gaped.

"My lands?" he echoed.

"Even so," said Penn.

"What?" He leapt forward. "Am I to have no reward?"

"The poor reward of thy life," averred the Lord Proprietor. "I misdoubt if it is deserved or if it benefits thee," he added, and briefly told the prisoner so much as seemed safe of what had been told me.

He that had been the Ranger shrieked. He tossed his arms in an ecstasy of imprecation. The burning building cast his silhouette against the trees beyond him, where it gyrated antics like a gigantic ape. Appeals were useless, and he knew it, but, when his paroxysm brought him face to face with Sir Geoffrey, he recognized in my friend the active agent of his downfall and straightway sought to drag that agent with him.

"Justice!" he yelled. "You call this justice, I war-

rant! Then what o' him, t'tyke?" Simon Scull had
been that near death, he must have still been smelling
of the grave, and yet, so strong is hatred, he would not
forego his vengeance. "Ye've heard tell how t'crown
jewels of England are these long year' missing, Thomas
Penn?" He pointed with a skinny claw. "This clout
has them on him now—t'highwayman!"

CHAPTER XXXV

HONOR AT STAKE

IT had come at last. I caught my breath. Not only was my friend's safety in the balance: those gems must be delivered to the Stuarts, or else it would be said that with them my father bought his freedom.

"Search him!" screamed Simon Scull, still pointing a clawlike finger. "Search him: they are there!"

All eyes were turned to Sir Geoffrey.

He brushed by his mad accuser. He stood before the Lord Proprietor and, flinging back his cloak, raised his hands above the singed curls of his head.

"No underling shall touch me," he declared; "but any gentleman may search—and then face me in fair fight."

Did he count on their fear of his sword? The chance of his counting too heavily frightened me.

"Search him!" repeated Simon. "Are ye all afeared?" He crept up. "I'll do't mysel'!"

Sir Geoffrey stopped him with a glare. "I said 'any gentleman.'"

"Hands off!" commanded the Proprietor. "And thee," he addressed Sir Geoffrey: "thy word of honor will suffice. Are, or are not, these jewels upon thee?"

On my protector's honor I would have ventured my

life. So now I looked either for him to surrender or make a fighting dash for liberty.

"They are not," said he.

My own eyes had seen him bestow them in his clothes. Though a lie meant his safety and the saving of my father's reputation, I sobbed aloud for this destruction of an idol.

Scarcely I heard Penn say that this was enough. Scarcely I heeded the dragging away of protesting Scull, who must be lodged in the Lancaster jail until proper assurances of a peaceful boundary-settlement should be obtained by our messenger to Annapolis. I went to the Proprietor.

"May I have a word with—with him?" And I nodded toward Sir Geoffrey, standing proudly now at a few yards' distance, and, it seemed, very much alone.

"Why not?" says Penn. "Thee's free, and he is also. But I do not deny that we dread his powers of persuasion, should they be employed again on thee.— Will thee give me a first word—Mr. Wright and me together?"

He could not be denied, nor the Magistrate beside him.

"When first I clapped eyes on thee in Philadelphia," continued the Proprietor, "I read thee for a likely lad, young as thee was—and young as thee is, thee's proved me correct. It's such as thee we need in Pennsylvania. Before thee passes for a moment under any other influence, I'd say to thee: remain here, away from kings, exiled or reigning. My part may take me elsewhere, but thee has life before thee, and, unless I misread the future, crowns will not long hold sway in the Americas."

"I shall remain," said I. "You have told me that my father is to come."

"I know—I know," he said; "but for thee I fear persuasion. His pardon will restore your father's wealth, yet his English lands were sold, and his title will not be restored with his riches." Penn's head turned ever so slightly in Sir Geoffrey's direction. "I feared lest some lure of winning back the title ——"

He stopped. When I saw that answer was not interruption, I replied:

"After these years, the title can mean little to my father. To me it means nothing."

Then Mr. Wright joined in, his stern lips softened and his deep-set eyes, too.

"Well said!" he cried. "And if they are to live in Pennsylvania, I believe that neither of them, father or son, will want any title save such as they may earn here from the esteem of their fellow-colonists."

So he gave me his hand and told me I was to dwell with him under his daughter's, Susannah's, care at "Hempfield" until my father should arrive and a new "Lynton" should be built.

"And those poor Shawanese of Uncle Simon's—

Billy and Iron Hatchet: they were no sharers in his crimes," said I.—" They will not be punished? "

" Someone saw them peeping from their quarters a moment since," said Mr. Wright: " when thee's ready, go and tell them they are now to work for thee."

I thanked him again. " And, sir," says I, " on the security of my step-uncle's property, which is to be my father's, will you advance me the sum of seven pounds? "

" For what purpose? " he asked.

I told him, and he, with a word of commendation, handed me the money.

Then there was yet one thing more:

" I should like the ferrymen to-night, sir."

Now Thomas Penn laughed outright. " This is a maker-of-terms, Friend John! " he cried to the Magistrate.

" Well, you see, sir," I explained, " we left two horses on Round Top. I like them both, but one of them I love."

So the Magistrate consented, and then he looked at the Proprietor.

" And now thee thinks safe those words with our cloaked ally? "

" I think them safe," said Penn.

Sir Geoffrey had moved away. I went to him with heavy steps, loath, for the first and last time, to speak with him, yet burthened by a heavy need.

He met me silently, his handsome, dark face inscrutable. Under the shadows of the roadside trees we passed.

"What is it, Nicky?" he then inquired. "What ails you, boy?"

"O Sir Geoffrey," I wailed, "I *saw* you take them!"

My grief overcame me. He laughed, and that he should have not even shame struck me a crueler blow.

"Why, Penn does not want them," said he, "and Wright would not touch them on any account: both those are Stuart men at heart—when not red republicans! Saw you not the gleam in their eyes when Scull accused me? It was that gleam I answered."

"Aye, but the truth—the truth!"

He frowned. "You doubt me?"

"How can I else?"

His hand went to his sword-hilt, but then he laughed again and shrugged in his French fashion.

"It was the truth I told them! I have not the jewels on my person, nor had for many a minute before the asking. Honest and resourceful Harley—Harley the servant, whom none will suspect: he is on his way to Philadelphia. There is a road from Philadelphia to New York, and every month a packet sails from New York for Italy." He clapped me on the shoulder. "Nicky—Nicky, lad—Rome is in Italy, and the head of the royal house of Stuart, the Chevalier de St. George, is in Rome: ten weeks hence, those gems will be in the possession of their rightful owner and my lawful sovereign!"

We had reached the horses that we had ridden from "Hempfield." He mounted one.

"Oh, I shall arrange for its return, young Honesty!" he said. "I follow Harley. Will you come along, Nicky?"

That was the sudden way he loved. My heart came into my throat: the ties that bound us were never stronger; but I shook my head.

"It must not be," said I. "My father is to come out here, and here my destiny is cast." Somehow I felt then, and for always, that this new land was to be my country—somehow realized that, despite all I had suffered here, I should one day love it. "For your sake, I should wish to go," I said; "but here is my home to be, and I neither King James's man nor yet the man of him they call King George."

He winced. He bent to me. In the shadows as we were, I could see him smile, and that the smile was sad, and he looking far older than his wont.

"Why, so the whole world goes," said he—there was the extent of the "persuasion" which the Lord Proprietor and his Magistrate had feared!—"and so even just causes and firm friendships cannot remain forever young. You are a brave lad anyways, and perhaps one that can see the more distant duty." Suddenly he put his arms about me. I was sure he would only make some high difficulty in knowingly accepting the return of his months' old loan to me, so, while still enfolded by his embrace, I slipped into a pocket of his cloak the seven pounds that I had got from the Lord Proprietor.

"Good-bye!" he cried, none the wiser for my action. Hatless he was, yet he executed at least the half-mocking flourish of one of his grand bows. He clapped his boot-heels into his horse's flanks. "Good-bye, American!"

The horse started. Over the sound of its hoofs, I heard Sir Geoffrey's voice ring high:

> "'Far away is he I love,
>   And who shall watch above him?
> Here are only those who hate—
>   And who is there to love him?
> Yet I wadna' (vows the Lass)
>   'Hae him aught but frae me,
> While a land that is his own
>   Owns no love for Jamie!'"

294